The House on Maple Street

By Heidi Slowinski

Published by Amazon Services LLC, 410 Terry Ave N, Seattle, WA 98109

Cover art by Maggie Duford

The House on Maple Street / Heidi Slowinski

p. cm

eISBN: 978-1-7343014-0-3

ISBN: 978-1-7343014-1-0

https://heidislowinski.com

To Meirah Rachel with much love

Table of Contents

Prologue

Evelyn could feel her pulse quicken as she started to read the article on the screen in front of her. She'd come in to work early so she could do a little research before she started for the day. The library was still closed, and she was the only one in the building. She enjoyed the peace of being able to work, uninterrupted. Given what she was now reading, the eerie stillness, surrounded by nothing but books, seemed fitting. Evelyn continued to scroll through the newspaper article on the microfiche reader.

There was a grainy, sepia photo from the accident scene. The headlights illuminated a curved, rural road lined with trees. Evelyn's mind drifted to taking a leisurely drive along a lane like that. The sun shining through the trees and the warm summer air blowing through her hair. Maybe this summer, she'd finally buy that vintage convertible she'd always wanted. She shook off the daydream as she returned to the article in front of her. Further down the page was a photo of a young woman smiling, posed affectionately with a bright-eyed little boy. Judging by the ages of the people in the photo, it must have been recent, taken not more than a few weeks before the accident.

Evelyn scrolled back to the top of the article. She always skimmed through a new article before she read it properly, checking the photos to make sure the story she was about to read was about the subject she was looking for. There was no doubt who the woman in the photo was. Evelyn was familiar enough with the Brown family to recognize her easily. She felt like she knew her. The little boy must be her son. The caption didn't give his name. His smile was sweet and mischievous. She smiled at him lightly before she started reading the article again.

Police were summoned to the scene of a fatal accident Friday night on a rural route, a few miles outside of town. A woman had been driving at a high rate of speed, without her headlights on. It was late, around 11pm. It rained earlier in the evening and the moon was obscured by clouds, making it especially dark. The road was still wet. She had taken a sharp curve way too fast, crossing the center line where she struck another car in a violent, head on crash. Her car traveled off the other side of the road and came to final rest at the bottom of a ravine. There was another photo Evelyn had overlooked. The car with its front end completely demolished. The windshield was shattered.

Evelyn took a sip of her coffee then reached for her notebook, where she kept a list of details about the Maple Street house to look into later. She jotted down a note about the little boy having been in the car at the time of the accident. There had been another article about him in what she'd found so far, but she hadn't been able to find his name. The family having such a common last name made finding accurate details more complicated. If he died in the accident, there must be an obituary out there somewhere. But for now, Evelyn wondered, what would make her decide to go out for a drive so late at night? Why was her son in the car and why were her headlights off? Evelyn continued reading hoping the article provided more details or at least a clue.

The car was severely damaged by the impact but there was evidence her brake lines had been cut, according to the investigators at the scene. Evelyn froze. She read this again, to be sure she read it right. There was evidence the car was tampered with. That the brake lines were cut before the accident happened. This accident wasn't an accident at all. Someone meant for her to crash.

The article went on about the Brown family. The grandfather of the young woman in the article had been a great philanthropist who left a substantial endowment to the college where Evelyn now worked. The library she was sitting in bore his name. He built the beautiful Victorian house where she rented a room. To say the Brown family had been well off was an understatement. Was that what motivated someone to want to harm her? Maybe whoever did this wasn't planning on the little boy being in the car. Evelyn's mind was racing with questions and speculation when she was startled by florescent lighting coming on overhead.

"Oh, I'm sorry, Ms. Berke," stammered her equally startled intern, "I didn't realize you were in already."

"That's alright, Nina," Evelyn replied annoyed, "I brought bagels in this morning. They're in the break room." Her tone softening but only a little. It was nearly eight o'clock. She'd have to get to work soon anyway but the interruption was still an annoyance.

"Wow! Thanks Ms. Berke," Nina exclaimed a little too brightly, especially considering Evelyn brought her interns bagels for breakfast every Friday morning. Evelyn rolled her eyes as she watched Nina's hasty retreat from the room.

Evelyn turned back to her article, skimming back over the part she'd already read to refresh her memory. Neighbors of the Brown family were interviewed. Nothing in the quotes provided Evelyn any useful information as to what she was doing out so late with her son or what she might have been running away from. There was no speculation at all. Each quote was a message of sympathy to the Brown family, comments about what a wonderful person she was, and how sweet her little boy was. Such a tragedy. She was so young. That poor little boy. Not a word about the circumstances surrounding the accident.

The lead investigator at the scene was interviewed further. At first, he'd wondered if her lights had been so badly damaged in the accident that they weren't working. But when he'd looked inside the car, he'd noticed they were shut off. They were in the process of looking the car over more closely which is when the cut brake line was discovered. There was no way she would have been able to stop. Police were still looking into the circumstances of the accident, according to the article. Then at the very end, finally a mention of the driver of the other car. He'd been taken from the scene to a hospital. His condition wasn't mentioned. No name or other details about him. Evelyn jotted this down in her notes too. Maybe his identity was a clue.

Evelyn sat back in her chair, taking another sip of her coffee, lingering a minute before she started work for the day. She'd have to come back to this later. The whole thing didn't make any sense. What was a young mother doing, driving down a dark road, with no headlights on? And with her young son in the car so late at night. Evelyn researched the people who had once occupied other historic homes around town but had yet to run across anything this seemingly salacious. There was clearly more to this story that wasn't being told in the article. The daughter of a well-known family dies in a suspicious accident. Evelyn was thrilled at the idea of uncovering this mystery.

1

She turned down the radio. It should be coming up on the right. She was starting school in two weeks and still hadn't gotten around to finding housing. Ever the procrastinator, Hillary Altman spent all morning apartment hunting and there weren't a lot of options, especially considering her grad student budget. She had a good feeling about this last place.

Hillary stopped along the curb in front of a sign that read Maple Street Boarding House. A crude, hand lettered notice on the window by the front door read, room for rent. She sat back in her car admiring the historic Victorian surrounded by a white picket fence. The leaves on the large maple tree in the front yard were showing signs of the changing season. Charming. That was what this neighborhood was. It was charming. The notice in Hillary's hand didn't give many details on the apartment and there were no pictures. But the rent was cheap. She might have enough left over at the end of the week for a cup of coffee now and then. It was walking distance to campus. This just had to be it.

The front porch wrapped around to the side of the house. What a perfect spot to enjoy a warm fall evening as she worked on her creative writing portfolio. She found herself hoping the available apartment wasn't a depressing room over a garage, in the back. Or worse yet, in a damp basement. A notice on the front door said to inquire at the back door. Hillary's heart started to sink. She walked around the porch to the back of the house. Hillary knocked at the back door, but no one answered. She hesitated before trying the knob. The hinges groaned as the door opened. The back entry to the house was a dimly lit landing. Hillary's optimism only continued to fade.

Another crudely hand lettered sign read simply, "landlord downstairs". Hillary hesitated a moment before opening the worn wooden door. The staircase was steep and old. There was a mustiness in the air. A single bulb burned at the bottom of the stairs, barely illuminating her way. Hillary made her way cautiously down, suddenly remembering every horror movie her ex-boyfriend insisted they watch together. This was how the attractive girl died, wasn't it? Foolishly taking directions from a crude sign and descending the dimly lit stairwell to the dank basement. She was suddenly certain she'd find some sort of torture chamber at the bottom of the stairs.

Instead, she encountered another sign. This one clearly purchased at an office supply store, judging by the block lettering. Hillary could feel herself start to relax. The lighting was better at the bottom of the stairs than it seemed from above. Or maybe her eyes just adjusted. She knocked below the sign that read, rental office. There was a clattering beyond the door. Someone cursed.

"I'm coming," rasped a male voice, followed by the sounds of a smoker's cough, thick and heavy with phlegm.

Hillary recoiled. She considered dashing back up the stairs. Maybe one of the other places she'd seen this morning would work out after all. Hillary could feel her weight starting to shift in retreat as the door in front of her opened.

"Yeah," he said, leaning heavily on the frame. The stench of stale alcohol radiating off this unkempt figure was so strong Hillary nearly wretched. Grease stains colored the stretched-out undershirt he wore. "Well, what do you want," he barked.

"Umm," Hillary stammered. "You have a room for let," she managed, holding out the page in her hand.

"Yeah," he responded gruffly. Hillary hesitated. "You want to see it?" he finally asked.

"Yes, please," she squeaked out.

"Hang on," said the overweight man. He left the door ajar as he turned back into the room beyond. Hillary stood uncertainly. She heard grumbling and more cursing. Something rattled followed by a crash and another curse. Then the shuffling steps coming back to the door. "Come on," he muttered, stumbling slightly as he moved past her to the stairs.

Hillary turned and followed him at a safe distance, holding her breath. They proceeded back to the landing, through another door that led to a kitchen. The man didn't speak as he moved toward the front of the house, to a center staircase. Hillary refrained from glancing right or left. They continued up to the second floor of the house. She could hear the man's breathing, heavy with the exertion. At the top of the stairs, they stopped. The man reached into the pocket of his ill-fitting, ripped jeans, producing a set of keys. He shuffled through them before placing one in the lock. Hillary allowed herself a nervous look around.

"This is it," the man finally said, pushing open the door for her.

Hillary cautiously stepped inside. She was greeted by the warm afternoon light, shining in through the windows of the second-floor turret, warming the hardwood floors. She felt herself finally relax as she took in the view of the quaint street below from the windows. It was perfect.

"Rent's due first of the month. There's parking in the back. If you want meals, it's an extra hundred a month. No pets allowed." His tone was well rehearsed.

Hillary didn't turn around when she said, "I'll take it".

The landlord's name, according to the lease agreement, was Keith. She couldn't read the last name and Hillary wasn't about to ask. She took the keys and handed over the deposit. The Maple Street Boarding House had five bedrooms for rent. The main floor rooms were for common use of the tenants. The extra rent covered breakfast and evening meals prepared by a housekeeper, the landlord referred to as Beatrice. Beatrice also handled the cleaning. Having never been very skilled at cooking, Hillary decided the convenience was worth the extra expense. There was a shared bathroom at the end of the hall. Hillary was instructed to work out the schedule of its use with the other tenants. She was relieved to hear there were other tenants and she wouldn't be occupying this house alone with her landlord.

Back downstairs, Keith showed her around the common rooms. The dining room was occupied by a large, antique table that reminded Hillary of an English country estate house. A small front room had a television and a shabby looking sofa. She marveled at the living room. It was in the first-floor turret room, below her own. Built-in bookshelves lined the walls around a fireplace and a piano sat near a conversational seating area.

"You like books?" Keith asked as she skimmed the bindings.

"Yes," she'd answered, "I'm getting my MA in fine arts at JC. I'm planning to become an author."

"Huh," Keith grunted. "One of those brainy chicks then." With this, he'd winked at her. Hillary wondered if any of the other tenants were home this time of day. "Bet you write them steamy romance books with the muscled-up men and chicks with the ripped tops on the cover." Hillary's skin crawled.

"No," she replied flatly. "I work in historical fiction." Keith didn't respond; probably not his genre.

She relaxed as she got back into her car, relieved to be away from him. It was the cheapest housing option available near campus. She didn't expect she'd be spending much time there. It was just a place to sleep. And how often does a tenant even see their landlord anyway? Even in a boarding house, she didn't expect she'd see him much.

Hillary couldn't wait to talk to her best friend, Rachel, later. To tell her about the amazing view from her windows. And she had a lot of packing to do.

2

The back stairs seemed steeper with every step. Were there more of them somehow? Hillary wished she had enlisted a friend or two to help out with moving into her apartment. Her parents said they would help, if they lived closer. But her mother wanted to see pictures of her new place, once she got settled in. Her parents retired to Florida two months after she started her undergraduate studies. They clearly hadn't intended on her ever needing to move back home again by their choice of downsizing to a two-bedroom condo on the beach. She'd visited for Passover, sleeping on a lumpy pullout sofa in their den. The second bedroom was a combination office and craft room. Hillary cringed at the memory of her mother trying to play matchmaker with the Cantor's son at their temple. Her mother had gone on and on about what a good boy he was and that she should keep an open mind. Right. Emphasis on boy. Her mother had never been much of a judge of age. The kid had hardly been *Bar Mitzvahed*. He'd awkwardly hovered around her through the whole *seder*.

Rachel laughed hysterically as Hillary told her the story, in their dorm room, after getting back to school the following week. Rachel then proceeded to regale Hillary with tales of her holiday spent in the company of some perfect med student. Or was it the chemical engineer PhD candidate this year? Not that it really mattered when it came to Rachel. She was always in the company of some seemingly perfect guy who would be promptly cast aside before things got too serious.

Hillary was snapped out of the memory by the cramping in her legs. She had to pick a second-floor walkup, didn't she? Her car was packed full. This was at least her tenth trip and she hadn't made so much as a dent. At least the furniture she ordered online was delivered for her the day before. It was cheap and she still had to put everything together. But it would serve while she was going to school. Now thinking about it, she probably should have started with setting everything up before unpacking her car. The boxes were just going to be in her way as she tried to assemble her bed frame and put together all the dresser drawers. It was a warm afternoon and she was sweating hard from hauling everything up those stairs. Maybe a break was in order after this trip. As she made her way down the hall, a sudden pocket of chilly air brushed Hillary's skin, like a breath of fresh air, as she struggled with the oversized box in her arms.

"That looks heavy," came a voice.

Hillary stopped, looking over the top of the box, into a pair of smiling blue eyes. He was tall and fit, in a khaki dress shirt and pants, crisply ironed. His brown shoes looked as though they had been shined.

"It is, actually," Hillary managed. This place suddenly had its merits. "I'm Hillary. I'm just moving into the front room."

"Nice to meet you, Hillary," he responded. "Robert."

Hillary awkwardly shifted the box to get a better grip, struggling slightly with the weight. Or maybe it was her own awkward nature at meeting her handsome new neighbor. She suddenly wished she had even an ounce of Rachel's confidence and ease when it came to meeting men. Rachel would know exactly what to say right now. She would probably have Robert carrying the rest of the boxes out of her car and setting up her furniture already. At the very least, she'd have him carrying this box she was struggling with. Rachel always seemed to ooze charisma and charm. The only thing Hillary was oozing right now was her own sweat. Something she was becoming even more aware of as she awkwardly tried to think of something to say.

"Have you lived here long," she finally asked, mentally kicking herself for the moronic question. Why did she have to be such an awkward klutz?

"I just moved in a few months ago," Robert responded, smiling casually.

"Oh, great," she responded a little too enthusiastically. Hillary's mind was blank, unable to think of a better reply. "Are you a student at JC too?" she asked.

"JC?" he asked, seeming puzzled. "I'm afraid I'm not familiar with it. I'm not a student, in any case."

"Oh," said Hillary, disappointed.

"If you'll excuse me, I'll let you get back to your unpacking. There's somewhere I have to be," Robert said, finally putting her out of her misery.

"Right, I should get back to it," she responded, shifting the box again. She was talking way too fast. "Well, I'm sure I'll see you around, Richard." Hillary froze at hearing her mistake. "Robert, I mean Robert. I am so sorry!" She laughed nervously. "Umm, it was really nice meeting you."

He stepped out of her way, with a smile, as she hurried down the hall to her room where she dropped the box more forcefully than she intended. Hillary put her hands on her hips and surveyed the disorganized mess around her.

"I am such an idiot," she whispered to herself.

3

Hillary finally took a break to get cleaned up before dinner. Her room was still a disaster. She had done battle with the bedframe for about an hour, but it was finally together. The drawers for her new dresser came with a set of instructions in a language she didn't even recognize. So far, she'd managed putting together two of them, using the diagrams. And she still hadn't finished unpacking her car. Hillary was relieved to find the bathroom was unoccupied and immaculately clean. She wanted nothing more than to sink into a hot bath in the claw foot tub, but she settled for a quick shower instead. A list of house rules she'd found posted on her door said dinner was served promptly at 6:30pm. She'd managed to locate a suitcase with some of her clothes, relieved it wasn't all workout gear. She wasn't sure if there was a dress code for dinner here, but she guessed yoga pants would probably be frowned upon.

She heard the door across the hall open and close at some point earlier in the afternoon. Or at least she thought she had. She was being bested by a dresser drawer at the time.

But she assumed the room across the hall was occupied. Other than Robert, she had yet to meet, or even see, any of the other tenants in the house.

Hillary heard a clattering of dishes as she made her way down the stairs. A warm glow radiated from the entry to the dining room. It looked so inviting and something smelled absolutely delicious. Dinner was laid out in chafing dishes across an antique buffet. A scholarly looking man stood at the buffet, placing sautéed string beans on his plate next to steaming mashed potatoes. Hillary's mouth started to water as she spotted the perfectly cooked brisket. She suddenly realized she hadn't eaten all day and she was famished.

"Ah, here she is," said a middle-aged woman seated at the table, pushing up her glasses. Hillary had been so preoccupied with the food she failed to notice the woman. "Getting settled in okay?" the woman asked in a friendly tone.

"Yes, thank you," Hillary responded, spotting a stack of plates at one end of the buffet.

"There you are, dear. I was just about to come looking for you." The plump woman just entered the room with a basket of what was almost certainly freshly baked rolls. Hillary could smell the warm, yeasty aroma. The woman reminded Hillary of her *bubbe*. "I'm Beatrice. I'm the housekeeper here." She set the basket on the table. "Don't be shy. You must be starving. Take a plate," she gestured toward the plates.

Hillary smiled politely as she crossed the room to the buffet, picked up a plate, cutlery and a napkin. This was far nicer than anything she'd expected when she elected to pay the extra fee for meals. It was the first time in she couldn't remember how long she'd sat down to a meal that wasn't takeout food or cooked in a microwave. Hillary selected the seat next to the woman in glasses. The gray-haired gentleman sat across from them. Beatrice set down glasses of water for each of them.

"I'm Evelyn," said the woman next to her. "I have the room across from the bathroom."

"Nice to meet you," Hillary replied. "I'm Hillary. Front turret room."

"Are you a student?" Evelyn asked. She wore twill pants and a soft, heathered, lavender Henley. Her blond hair was pulled back in a low bun.

"Yes, I'm starting a fellowship at JC. I write historical fiction. Or at least I'm hoping to."

Evelyn smiled. "I'm the head librarian there, she said passionately. "I expect we'll see a lot of each other. If you need any help finding your way around, just let me know." Hillary could sense an immediate kindredship to Evelyn.

"Thank you. I'll keep that in mind," said Hillary savoring a bite of the deliciously tender brisket.

"I'm David Immerman. Doctor David Immerman," interjected the man across the table, placing strong emphasis on his title. "I'm head of the history department at JC and your neighbor across the hall."

Hillary smiled at him with a slight nod. He had a pompous air about him. She'd have to be conscious not to make too much noise. He seemed the type who would complain about that sort of thing.

"I hope I didn't disturb you this afternoon," Hillary offered.

"No," he responded flatly, not elaborating further.

Hillary turned back to Evelyn. "Have you lived here long?"

"I've been here about five years now," she responded. "I relocated from a small town in the mid-west I can promise you, you have never heard of. Needed a fresh start. Long story. I won't bore you. I fell in love with the charm of the town."

"You said you're a librarian. Do you also write?" Hillary asked, feeling a little more at ease.

"I dabble here and there but I spend most of my spare time doing research for the historical society. I leave the writing to other members. I'd rather be credited in someone else's work than having to spend time promoting and marketing my own."

"That makes sense," responded Hillary. It didn't really make much sense to Hillary at all. Giving someone else the credit for her work sounded like a waste but it felt like the right thing to say. "Do the rest of the tenants not take their meals here?" Hillary asked, changing the subject. She was disappointed at not seeing Robert at dinner. She hoped to make a better second impression after their awkward first encounter.

"We are the only tenants in the building," responded Dr. Immerman abruptly. Hillary didn't expect she would be welcome to call him David.

"Really?" Hillary asked. "I met someone named Robert earlier today when was I moving in. I think he's in the room next to the bathroom."

Evelyn studied her a minute. "He must have just moved in. I didn't realize Keith was renting out that room. It hasn't been occupied in the entire time I've lived here."

"And Keith doesn't take his meals here?" asked Hillary hoping the answer would be in the negative. She was in no hurry to see him again.

"Oh, gracious no," laughed Evelyn. "Other than showing apartments, he rarely leaves the basement. Thank goodness," she added. "Do yourself a favor and steer clear of Keith," Evelyn warned but didn't say any more as Beatrice came into the room with a carafe of coffee and a decadent looking cake. The three around the table remained silent as

Beatrice sliced the cake and retrieved coffee cups from a cupboard in the buffet.

"How's the dinner?" Beatrice asked finally breaking the silence.

"Delicious," Hillary answered brightly. Her fellow tenants nodded in agreement.

"Thank you, Beatrice," added Dr. Immerman.

Beatrice removed one of the chafing dishes and left the room.

"Coffee?" asked Evelyn as she got up from the table.

"Yes, please," responded Hillary as she finished the last bite from her plate. She felt stuffed but the cake was too tempting to pass up. They settled into their coffee and dessert.

"Tell me more about this person in the room next to the bathroom," Evelyn asked.

"Well I only met him for a minute, but I think he'd said he has been living here a few months already," Hillary started, feeling the color starting to rise in her cheeks. Evelyn's mouth curled slightly.

"Well he clearly made an impression on you," Evelyn teased, sipping her coffee.

4

Evelyn skimmed through real estate records on her lunch break. Although it was mind numbing reading, she found it relaxing. Piecing together a history of the ownership of a property gave her breadcrumbs to follow. It also gave her a timeline to work from when looking for other information. She usually started with this when working on a new property. She hadn't had much time to work on this project lately. Classes would be starting soon. The freshman class was due to start moving in that weekend. There were new books to catalog, interns to train, welcome materials to post around the library. She was beginning to drive herself crazy with her own perfectionism. It was time for a much-needed break.

According to the property tax records Evelyn was reviewing, the house had been owned by the Brown family, dating back to the early 1900s. Its original owner had been William Brown Senior. There was a new ownership record in 1918 that also belonged to a William Brown. But on digging a little further, Evelyn discovered this William Brown was William

Brown Junior, likely son of William Brown Senior. In Evelyn's experience, this usually meant there had been a death and the property changed hands by inheritance. She made note of the date. From what she already knew of William Brown Senior, he passed away sometime around 1917 or 1918. The title on the house changed to his son in 1918. She would need to do a little more digging to firm up the dates around this. With William Senior being such a well-known philanthropist in this area, there should be plenty of articles about him, especially around the time of his death.

So far, there was nothing unusual to catch Evelyn's attention in the history of the house. Another member of the historical society mentioned the place having a storied past when Evelyn discussed taking on this project, at a meeting, a few months ago. From what Evelyn knew William Brown Senior died of natural causes. And he hadn't been a young man by the standards of the time period. So far, nothing seemed out of the ordinary.

Evelyn kept scrolling through the records. The next change of title did stand out. The house was transferred to a bank in the 1950s. Evelyn jotted down the date. It seemed a little unusual that a house, owned by the same family for over fifty years, would suddenly be foreclosed on. She did not remember ever hearing anything about a loss of the family fortune, bad investments, or of, say, William Junior having a pension for gambling. And a scandal of that nature would certainly be part of town folklore. Evelyn made note of this too. Maybe it would be worthwhile to set up a coffee date with that woman from the historical society. Evelyn remembered her mentioning having been Billy's, as she'd referred to him nostalgically, date to a dance or social, or something back in the day. Evelyn written the woman off as an attention seeking busybody at first, but she might know something useful if she was acquainted with the family back then.

The house had apparently been vacant after the title transferred to the bank. It hadn't changed again until about eight years ago when her current landlord purchased the house. Beatrice told her that the house had been undergoing a restoration project. That is, until Keith ran out of funds and ended up opening the house to boarders to try to bring in revenue to cover the rest of the repairs. Evelyn had been the only tenant for a few months before David moved in. Beatrice used to take dinner with her, to keep her company. Evelyn would have felt awkward eating alone and she enjoyed Beatrice's company. This stopped when David moved in. Evelyn preferred Beatrice's company to his. David was a stodgy old miser with the personality of a wet dish rag. According to Beatrice, Keith had apparently intended to sell the house at a substantial profit. Some get rich quick plan that obviously fizzled. Evelyn had been living in the back bedroom, overlooking what were the gardens, for the past five years but had yet to see Keith lift a finger to do anything by way of repair or restoration. It had taken him three months to fix the dripping faucet in the bathroom. Evelyn doubted she'd need to find other housing any time soon.

The local newspaper was more of a newsletter and likely would have covered the sale of the house. Not much happened in such a small town. Evelyn did a little searching and found an article about the most recent sale of the house. After much petitioning by a group of local residents, the bank holding title to the Maple Street house finally decided to put the home up for auction. It confirmed Evelyn's assumption. The house had been vacant since the Brown family abandoned it in the fifties. No mention, in the article, of why they left. She was definitely going to have to make that coffee date. The group petitioning for the bank to finally put the house up for sale had been raising funds to purchase it. They intended to open the historic home as a museum. The plan fell through when Keith, with unnamed backers, showed up to the auction and managed to easily outbid the group. There were quotes in the article, hoping the developer who purchased the house, would consider their intended purpose. Or maybe of convincing him to donate it to them.

"Like that was going to happen," Evelyn mused aloud, rolling her eyes.

Others suggested taking legal action to have the house added to a historic homes registry to prevent the new buyer from gutting the place.

"Little did they know, the new buyer was not that ambitious," Evelyn snickered.

Evelyn glanced at the clock. She needed to get back to work. She'd have to pick this up later. Something happened in the fifties that caused the Brown family to abandon the Maple Street house. Considering its value, it had to be something huge to cause them to simply walk away. Evelyn skimmed through her notes to be sure she had all of the names and dates she'd found thus far. She also jotted a note about scheduling coffee with the woman from the historical society who knew the Brown family.

5

"Let's get that mess off your face, sweetie. We have to be neat and tidy when Daddy gets home, don't we?" A young woman knelt in front of the little boy, wiping his face with her fingers as Hillary came in from the back yard. The woman wore an A-line dress, the skirt spread around her on the floor. The sandy haired little boy stood perfectly still, allowing the procedure. His button-down shirt was tucked into his pair of shabby pants.

Hillary spent the morning at the library, lost in the short story she was writing before she'd gone to her class. Her first few weeks of school had been hectic, just trying to find a routine. But now she was settling into her schedule. She came home to relax before dinner. Roast chicken was on the menu tonight, Hillary's favorite. Later, she would head out to a poetry reading at a coffee shop a few blocks away. Hillary was surprised to see the woman and little boy in the house. As far as she knew there were no other tenants set to move into the house. Her neighbors didn't generally have visitors that she was aware of. Especially not at this time of the day.

"Excuse me," Hillary said when the woman didn't notice her entrance. Startled, the woman looked up at Hillary from where she knelt on the floor. Her soft brown eyes were wide with fear. "I'm so sorry! I didn't mean to scare you," Hillary apologized. The woman didn't relax.

"What time is it," she asked. Her auburn hair was perfectly coiffed in softly sculpted curls.

"I'm not sure exactly," Hillary responded. "Maybe around 4:30 or 5:00, I think."

"That late already? My goodness," the woman replied in a rushed tone. "I'll have to hurry." She returned to wiping at the little boy's face. This time more forcefully. The child's eyes didn't leave the woman in front of him. He didn't move or attempt to protest.

"I don't think we've met before. I'm Hillary," she introduced herself.

The woman didn't respond or acknowledge Hillary. She carried on smoothing the little boy's shirt, checking that it was securely tucked into his pants.

"Do you live here, in the house?" Hillary tried again.

"I'm Dottie," the woman finally replied. "This is my son, Tommy."

"I'm six," Tommy declared proudly, apparently deciding his mother's introduction was permission to speak.

"It's very nice to meet you, Tommy," Hillary smiled at him. He returned the gesture. One of his teeth was missing leaving a gap in his wide grin.

"Are you looking for Beatrice?" Hillary tried again. "She's usually working on dinner around now. I can find her for you."

"Oh no," declined Dottie. "There's no need to disturb her. We have to be on our way. My husband will be upset if his dinner is late."

Hillary was confused. Was she dreaming all this? Something about it didn't feel quite real to her. The woman either had to have a key or have been let in by someone else in the house. The door into the kitchen was locked when Hillary came in. She seemed to know who Beatrice was when Hillary mentioned her name, yet she didn't want to see her. It didn't seem she was there visiting Beatrice. And no attempt by Hillary uncovered any useful information as to who this woman was. Hillary was debating asking a more direct question when the woman rose up from the floor, taking her son by the hand.

"Come along, Tommy. Daddy will be home very soon," she said and moved toward the door to the basement stairs. Hillary hadn't noticed the door was ajar when she came in and she felt a cool rush of air as Dottie and her son passed through it. Hillary stood and watched as Dottie and Tommy disappeared down the basement stairs.

Hillary stood where she was in utter disbelief. Dottie's husband would be home soon, and she had to get dinner ready. That was what she said, wasn't it? Dottie took her son by the hand and said his daddy would be home soon. And then she'd gone down the basement stairs. Hillary milled this over in her head unable to rationalize it. Tommy's daddy was Keith?! Hillary wasn't sure what was more shocking to her in that moment. The fact that her disgusting landlord was married to a woman who looked like an old-world film star. That he apparently had a six-year-old son. Or the fact that she'd been living in the Maple Street house for the past three weeks without realizing there was a six-year-old child living in the basement. There were never any toys left in the yard. She'd never heard a child's voice in the house. No little feet running on the back stairs.

Hillary shook off the encounter and started up the back stairs. She had something more important to overthink for the time being. She hadn't run into Robert since the day she moved in. But today she finally had a plan. He didn't take meals with the other tenants where she could run into him. So today, she was going to be bold. She was going to knock on his door and invite him to join her for the poetry reading. This would be perfect. They'd have a chance to talk on the walk to the coffee shop, but it wasn't so far away that she would run out of things to talk to him about. And they could talk about the performances after, on the walk back home. Her inner romantic hoped it would be cool tonight. Maybe he would lend her his jacket. She rolled her eyes at this thought, reminding herself life was not a romantic comedy. But her plan was perfect! It was finally her turn to go out with the attractive, seemingly perfect guy.

She could feel her heart starting to race as she approached his door. Was she really going to do this? Her pace slowed as she got closer. She was really going to walk up to his door, knock, and ask him out. This was completely crazy! She never did things like this. Hillary took a deep breath, trying to calm herself down. This was no big deal. It was just a conversation. Just asking another human being to do a regular, everyday thing. After all, Rachel did this kind of thing all the time. It was no big deal. She took another deep breath. Hillary was standing in front of his door. She hesitated as she started to raise her hand. One more breath. She did it. She knocked.

Nothing.

Hillary listened a little more closely. There were no sounds coming from behind the door. Her anticipation and anxiety shifted to disappointment. What if he was sleeping and didn't hear her knock? She decided to try one more time. She knocked again. A little louder this time.

Nothing.

Hillary waited a bit longer. Her excitement completely vanished; her smile gone from her face.

He must have gone out, she assumed as she turned away from the door and continued down the hall to her own room. She sighed with the disappointment. So much for her brilliant plan. Maybe she could try again after dinner. He might be back in by then.

6

Hillary collected the book she had been reading from the desk in her room. There was time for a little reading before dinner. The fireplace in the living room was usually lit in the evenings now. The thought of sitting in front of a fire with her book before dinner cheered her up a little. As she came down the main stairs, she could hear the sounds of Beatrice preparing dinner in the kitchen. The aroma of roast chicken and lemons wafted down the hallway. At least dinner wouldn't be a disappointment.

The fireplace was burning brightly as Hillary walked into the living room. Dr. Immerman had also apparently decided to get in a little reading before dinner. He was seated in one of the wingback chairs, in front of the fireplace. Hillary hoped to be alone but Dr. Immerman wasn't exactly chatty.

"Good evening," he said as Hillary sat down opposite him, looking up from his book.

"Good evening," Hillary replied, echoing his formality. She opened her book, not expecting the conversation to continue.

"Lovely afternoon, today. Did you get a chance to enjoy the weather?" he continued.

"Umm, no not really. I was at the library this morning and then I had a class," Hillary responded. Her book was open to her page, in her lap.

"Hmm," was all he replied.

Hillary took up her book, expecting the conversation was now over. She struggled a bit to find her focus as she started to read. She was still thinking about her encounter with Dottie and Tommy. She found herself listening now. A six-year-old little boy couldn't be expected to keep silent all the time. And she knew the house wasn't well sound proofed. She could hear Dr. Immerman and Evelyn coming and going at various hours. Even now, she could hear Beatrice in the kitchen. Maybe the din from the kitchen was covering any sounds that might be coming from the basement. But to Hillary's imaginings, at least a portion of Keith's apartment should be just below where she and Dr. Immerman were sitting now. How had she never realized Keith had a family living with him? Her thoughts were interrupted by Dr. Immerman.

"Are you getting settled in around campus alright?" he asked. Hillary was surprised. Dr. Immerman had never taken any interest in her before.

"I am, thank you," she answered politely. Hillary considered her book a moment. She wondered again if she should try knocking on Robert's door after dinner, before she left for the coffee shop. By now, though, her earlier confidence had left her. She'd have to think of some other way to see him. Then it occurred to her Dr. Immerman seemed to be waiting for her to say something more. She quickly thought of something to ask him in return. "How long have you lived here, Dr. Immerman?"

"About five years," he responded. He didn't elaborate.

Hillary wondered if he might know something of Keith's wife and son, given he lived her so long.

"I met Dottie and Tommy on my way in this afternoon," she stated, unsure of how to start the conversation. Dr. Immerman studied her but he didn't respond.

"Oh," he said finally.

"They were in the kitchen when I came in this afternoon," she explained. He considered her again.

"Am I supposed to know who that is?" he asked. Hillary looked at him a long moment.

"I'm sorry. I assumed with you having lived here so long, you might know something about Keith's family," she explained.

"To be honest, I can't say that I have ever taken any particular interest in Keith or his family," replied Dr. Immerman.

Hillary didn't know how to respond to this. Dr. Immerman usually kept to himself and was not someone Hillary would ever describe as warm or particularly friendly. So it didn't seem that unusual that he wasn't acquainted with Dottie or Tommy. Hillary couldn't imagine Dr. Immerman taking an interest in a child. She had a hard enough time imagining him working with undergraduate students much less a six-year-old. She decided not to press the topic further.

"As I understand it, Keith has something of a colorful background. I'm not familiar with the story exactly. Someone helped him financially with the purchase of this house. I'm not sure who. I didn't care to ask. I don't believe the deed is in his name because of some trouble he was in a few years before he bought it. Something like that. Ms. Berke may know something more about it. I think that research project she's mentioned has something to do with this house. I don't generally pay attention when she talks." Dr. Immerman's manner of speaking was apathetic. Hillary found herself wondering if this man had any true passion about anything in life. "You would do well to avoid him, from what I understand," he added.

The corners of Hillary's mouth turned up slightly in acknowledgement of Dr. Immerman's warning. Evelyn said the same thing about Keith, at dinner, on her first night in the house. It never occurred to Hillary that she might need to do a background check on her landlord before choosing her housing for school. Maybe she should have. Hillary and Dr. Immerman settled into an awkward silence that was soon interrupted by Beatrice.

"Dinner is out on the buffet. Dish up while it's hot," she encouraged. Dr. Immerman didn't look up from his book.

Hillary smiled at her warmly. "Thank you, Beatrice. It smells delicious."

"Thank you, dear," she responded, smiling at Hillary's appreciation. "I know roast chicken is your favorite." With this she turned back toward the kitchen to prepare the coffee and dessert.

Hillary welcomed the interruption and call to dinner. She quickly got up from her chair and made her way to the dining room.

7

Evelyn was restless. She glanced at the clock. Quarter after mid-night. She got out of bed and went down to the kitchen. Beatrice always left the light above the stove on. Maybe a cup of chamomile would help. She put the kettle on the stove. The house was completely still. She honestly worried a little on hearing that a student was moving into the front room. But there was a definite difference between undergraduates and graduate students. Hillary seemed sweet, if not a little naïve. She puzzled over the tenant Hillary mentioned taking the room across from her own. Evelyn still hadn't seen or heard any sign of anyone occupying the room next to the bathroom. Maybe it was just a showing. But hadn't Hillary said he'd been living there a few months when she moved in? She carried her steaming cup carefully back up the back stairs.

Back in her room, Evelyn settled into an oversized chair in the corner of her room, near the windows. She pulled a plush fleece throw over her lap and picked up a file from the side table. It was clippings assembled by a committee with the historical society when they hoped to reopen the Maple Street house as a museum. They planned to provide brochures with a history of the house and the Brown family. No one bothered to finish writing the brochures, but the assembled articles might help her answer a few of her questions. The contents of the file were in disarray. Most of it was scans, printed out, from other sources.

The first article on the pile was a scanned copy across three sheets of paper. She slipped the paperclip from the corner. The article announced William Brown Senior and his wife started building a large house on Maple Street. The couple planned an elegant Victorian with surrounding gardens in the English style. The article was from 1901. The light fixtures were being handmade and imported from Italy, as was the stone to accent the fireplace. Evelyn recalled the stonework around the fireplace, in the living room, downstairs. It was beautiful but in need of a good cleaning. She also considered the light fixtures around the house. Those had obviously been replaced at some point after the house's construction. The originals would be worth a fortune today. Maybe the family did have some financial crisis and the fixtures were sold. The current fixtures around the house were certainly old but they weren't handcrafted in Italy, at the turn of the century, old. She made a note of this and took a sip of her tea.

The next article Evelyn picked up was about a social gathering being hosted by William Brown Junior and his wife.

It was dated 1919. The tone of the article gave the impression the house changed hands to Mr. Brown's son at some point prior. The party to be hosted was a fundraiser but the article was cut off before the cause was mentioned. There was a photo of William Brown Junior, young, tall, and slender. He was smartly dressed in the fashion of a gentleman of the time. His wife had dark hair and a sweet smile. Their little girl was also in the picture. She couldn't have been more than two or maybe three. She had her mother's dark hair. Her high-necked dress had puffed sleeves. Tucked in her arm was an expensive looking doll, wearing a matching dress. The family was posed on the front steps of the Maple Street house. Evelyn studied them a minute longer before making some notes.

Evelyn set this page aside. She'd organize this mess later. The next page announced the opening of the Maple Street house for public viewing. It had been completed in 1918. The article confirmed that it was originally built by William Brown Senior but was not completed before his passing in late 1917. His son, William Brown Junior oversaw the completion of the house and was intending to move in with his wife and young daughter. Admission was being charged at a nickel per person. According to the article, lemonade and refreshments would be served. Evelyn mused at the entry fee. She glanced back through the article. There was no mention of what the proceeds from the viewing were being used for.

Evelyn made note of this. The house had been bedecked with expensive finishes. William Brown Senior left a large endowment to the college at the time of his passing. And his son was opening the house to public tours, charging an admission, shortly after his father's death. Maybe the son was in financial difficulty. His father left behind a large, expensive, yet unfinished house. It took nearly two decades to complete the construction on the place. He'd also seemingly left the bulk of his fortunate to a small, private college. It stood to reason all of this could have been taxing on Junior's finances. In which case, he should probably be charging more, Evelyn smirked. Or was father concerned his fortune would be squandered by an irresponsible son, so he elected to give it away?

Evelyn made note of some questions she needed to dig into further. William Junior's wife was well dressed and looked considerably younger than him. Evelyn wondered what her background was. Was she from a good family, as they said? Or did she marry up? And their daughter was elegantly dressed for such a young child. The doll she was holding had to have cost a small fortune. Did years of overspending drive William Brown Junior into financial ruin? Evelyn sipped her tea as she studied the Brown family photo again.

Evelyn put the file aside and took up her notes. She had a good timeline on the ownership of the house and a few details about the past owners. But there was clearly a bigger story here. Now she had to figure out what it was.

8

Hillary sat at her desk. It was getting late. She should really go to bed, but she wanted to get a little more writing done before her meeting with her advisor the next day. She sat at her desk, in front of the windows, overlooking the street. The streetlamps glowed warmly in the mist outside. Hillary stared over the top of her laptop, studying the view, hoping for inspiration. Nothing was coming to her. Her mind was wandering and refused to focus. The poetry reading had been a huge disappointment.

She was looking for a mellow, low key vibe. A dimly lit room. People in pairs huddled together at small tables, sipping from stemless glasses of white wine, whispering to each other in their own little worlds. Something intimate, sophisticated, a little seductive even. That's what she had been in the mood for. And Robert. She had been hoping to be one of those pairs, whispering with Robert. Getting lost in each other at a table in a back corner somewhere. Maybe she would let herself be persuaded to get up and perform one of her own pieces. She imagined he'd be mesmerized, listening to her.

Then she'd take his arm as they strolled back to the house at the end of the night. Snuggling just a little closer to keep warm against the chilly fall evening under the stars. Perfect.

Her night had been the exact opposite. For starters, Robert hadn't answered the door when she knocked to invite him out. She went after dinner, leaning in and listening carefully. There were no sounds coming from inside to give hope that he was there. It was already dark outside, but no glow of lights came from under the door. He clearly wasn't in. So she walked alone to the coffee shop. Instead of a calm night filled with stars, it was cloudy, and she'd been fighting gusts of wind as she made her way down the street. Her hair had been whipped around and she was freezing by the time she reached the coffee shop. There wasn't much ambiance in the place. It was bright as noon. The performers were lively and the crowd noisy. People were clustered in large groups around the small café tables. The place was packed. She ordered a cup of tea and found a chair in a corner. She hadn't known a soul in the place. Hillary felt people looking at her, but no one greeted her. She finished her tea and walked home early, fighting back tears in the gusting wind.

Hillary's mood hadn't recovered much from that evening and it was being reflected in her writing, that was, when she could manage to put anything down on paper at all. She was well behind her goal for her meeting tomorrow. She had to muscle through and get something done. Hillary glanced at the blank screen on her laptop, then back out at the damp night. She was going to need caffeine if she was going to get anything done. And maybe another piece of Beatrice's unbelievable apple cake, if there was any left. She was wearing her favorite slouchy lounge pants, a tank top, and an oversized cardigan. Her hair was in a messy knot on top of her head. Any make-up she'd had on was long gone by now. She avoided the mirror above her dresser as she stepped into her slippers. She wasn't likely to run into any of her neighbors this time of night anyway.

Hillary pulled her cardigan a little tighter around herself as she made her way down the dimly lit hallway, toward the back stairs.

"Hi-de-ho," said Robert, startling Hillary out of her focus on her late-night snack. Her skin prickled. Of course she would run into him when she looked like this.

"Hi," she responded in surprise.

"I didn't expect to see anyone else up this time of night," he said. Hillary's mind drifted to imagining him sitting next to her in a dark café, at a small table. Staring into those eyes, the perfect shade of blue. She snapped back, hoping she hadn't left too long a pause.

"I was trying to get some work done and decided to go get a snack," Hillary explained, mentally congratulating herself for putting together a normal, coherent sentence. And simultaneously kicking herself for not getting dressed before venturing out of her room.

"A snack," he repeated. She couldn't read his facial expression.

Before Hillary could overthink his response, she blurted, "I was going to see if there was any more of Beatrice's apple cake. It is so good." She placed a long emphasis on the word so. Too long, she thought, kicking herself. So much for normal. Robert smiled at her but didn't say anything in response.

She could feel her anxiety rising. This was her chance to redeem herself from their first meeting. He was so good looking. His dark hair was slightly wavy. Hillary imagined running her fingers through it. She hoped she wasn't biting her lip. Why couldn't she just have a normal conversation with this guy? Her mind started to race as she tried to think of something else to say to him. This should be so simple. She watched Rachel do it all the time. And after all, he was just a person. What was the big deal? She suddenly realized they'd been standing in silence for a long time. Too long. She had to say something.

"Are you hungry? You could come down to the kitchen with me," she finally suggested.

"Thank you but it is very late," he replied. "You enjoy your cake, Hillary."

"Okay," she answered. "Maybe some other time then." She turned to go. "Good night," she added over her shoulder. Robert didn't respond.

Hillary made her way cautiously down the back stairs to the kitchen. Something about this house, at night, felt a little creepy. She was always a little afraid of running into Keith late at night. She was relieved to find the kitchen empty in the glow of the light over the stove. She was even more relieved to find the cake keeper was not empty. She fixed a coffee and a plate before going back up to her room.

An overwhelming sense of disappointment washed over Hillary as she passed Robert's door again. The lights were already off and all was quiet. A seemingly perfect guy just down the hall and she was blowing the opportunity with her social ineptitude. She really needed to talk to Rachel.

9

"Okay so tell me more about this guy you can't shut up about. Because I know that's all you want to talk about right now." Hillary was video chatting with her best friend, Rachel. They set a weekly check in schedule since going their separate ways, after graduation.

Rachel had been accepted to an elite graduate program after they finished college. She was one of those people who always had perfect grades but never seemed to study. Hillary, by contrast, had to fight for every grade and had barely been accepted to JC. Rachel decided she didn't want to pursue grad school or adulthood, in general, really. Instead, after college, she packed up her life and took off to a horse farm in Arizona. She spent her days guiding groups of tourists on trail rides. She seemed incredibly happy. Hillary envied her.

"I've only met him a couple of times, but he is the most perfect human being I have ever laid eyes on," Hillary gushed. "He has dark, wavy hair and the deepest blue eyes ever. I think he's in the army or something. He's been wearing a uniform whenever I've seen him."

"So, do you think he's into you?" Rachel asked bluntly.

Hillary stopped. She hadn't really considered if Robert was interested in her. She certainly wanted him to be. She wanted him to be crazy about her, to want to do all the little romantic gestures men really only did in the movies. But Hillary was so busy fantasizing about Robert, she hadn't really considered reality.

"Hil, is he into you? You're suddenly a million miles away. It's a simple question," Rachel demanded, interrupting her thoughts.

"Umm, I mean. He seems really nice and he's crazy good looking. I think I really just need to get to know him better." Hillary hoped she was convincing Rachel with this. She wasn't really convincing herself now that she was hearing it out loud.

"Okay, stop avoiding my question. I get that he's super handsome and all that. Which is lovely and all. But Hil, is he into you?" Rachel asked again. Her tone was growing more demanding.

Hillary felt like she was under interrogation and Rachel wasn't going to let it go until she answered the question. Robert stopped her in her tracks when she met him, moving into the house. And he looked so good the other night when she bumped into him. But now thinking back on it, she realized, he had hardly spoken to her. He didn't offer to help her when she was clearly struggling, moving in. The other night, he brushed her off when she asked him to go down to the kitchen with her. Of course, he didn't take his meals in the house so maybe he felt like he wasn't allowed to go down to the kitchen. And it was really late. His lights had been off by the time she came back upstairs. He could have just been really tired. Not to mention, she looked like a hot mess both times.

"To be fair, I haven't exactly looked my best the two times I've met him. The first time was when I was moving in. I looked completely disgusting. And the other night, I looked like a total slob in slouchy pants and my hair was in a top knot. I don't know how anyone looks cute in those," Hillary was rambling.

"Hil, oh my god," Rachel interrupted her. "This isn't about how you looked when you met him. You're clearly super into this dude. You've been blowing up my phone about him for weeks. But it sounds like he's giving you no reason to be into him at all. What kind of jerk doesn't offer to help someone, not just because you're a woman but, anyone who is struggling?! And you didn't ask him to go out clubbing at one am, the other night. You asked him to get a cup of tea. In your kitchen. Downstairs. No one is that tired."

Hillary really didn't want to hear any of this. She had been obsessively texting Rachel about Robert since she first met him. She had idealized him. She knew it. But it hurt to have to face it.

"*Chica*, seriously. You need to get past this and go meet a nice boy your *bubbe* can brag about at *mahjong*," Rachel teased. Hillary laughed.

"What, like you? How are things with your David of the month these days?" Hillary shot back, sarcastically. "Or have you moved on to Juans and Joses now? And when did you start learning Spanish?!"

"Sorry, *yelda*." Rachel retorted with a sarcastic laugh. "But you know I'm right. And his name is Miguel, if you must know."

"Oh my god," Hillary laughed, rolling her eyes. "Seriously, what is wrong with you?"

"A question my 'smother' asks on a biweekly basis," Rachel responded. Her mother had always had impossibly high expectations for Rachel. Expectations Rachel utterly obliterated when she'd taken off to ride horses in the southwest. Rachel's studio apartment was even above the stable. Her mother had been mortified the first time she'd seen it.

"Are you seriously dating some guy you met on the farm?" Hillary asked, still laughing.

"He's a veterinarian," Rachel responded in a matter of fact tone. Hillary just shook her head. "It's nothing serious." It never was with Rachel. "But he's really fun to be around."

"And who's to say Robert isn't fun to be around? This could be a nice change for me. I could do 'it's not that serious'," Hillary argued.

"Hillary, you know I love you. But no, you can't," Rachel replied. She wasn't laughing anymore. "You're not an 'it's not that serious' kind of girl. You're the old soul who needs the romantic fairytale of the nice boy, with the nice career, who proposes at the nice restaurant, so you can have the nice wedding, under the nice *chuppah*. And the two of you can build the nice home, with your nice kids, and live your nice life. It's one of the things I love about you. You don't settle. So don't settle."

If it was possible to feel homesick for a person, Hillary felt it for her best friend right then. Rachel was right. She knew Rachel was right. Normally, right now, they would crack open a couple of pints of ice cream and binge watch something mindless until she felt better. But her best friend was thousands of miles away, riding horses, and learning Spanish from a veterinarian named Miguel, apparently. After they signed off for the night, Hillary curled up on her bed and cried.

10

Hillary had a restless night. She cried herself to sleep last night. When she'd woken up, around two thirty, she'd gone down the hall to the bathroom. She's held a damp, cool cloth against her eyes for a while. She could take her time. The rest of the house was quiet. Everyone was asleep. And this time, she was happy to not run into Robert.

Robert, all of this was because of Robert. How was it that a guy she met all of twice could make such a mess of her? Had she seriously cried herself to sleep over him? She was mourning like she had been dumped. By a guy she had never gone out with. Not even once. It was all she could think about as she'd finally climbed back into bed. She finally managed to get back to sleep a little after four. She didn't have any classes or meetings all day, so she could have stayed in bed. But her eyes shot open about five and that was the end of her night. Hillary checked her reflection, after getting dressed. She looked exhausted. And the cool cloth did nothing to control the puffiness of her eyes. Hillary decided not to bother with make-up. She'd get something for breakfast and maybe take a walk or something. She really needed a solid workday if she didn't want to get further behind.

There was a small part of her that was mad at Rachel. What right did she have to be so opinionated about Robert?! Rachel had never met Robert. No, Rachel had to go running off to Arizona. They were supposed to be doing this together. That was their agreement since junior year. They would apply to the same school and get a cheap two bedroom somewhere. Rachel gave her no warning when she'd changed her plans. She had seen some random post online somewhere about a job opportunity and just like that, she was packing her stuff. Hillary was crushed. And now, here was Rachel with all these opinions about what she should and shouldn't do. Who she should and shouldn't date. Who was she to get an opinion? She left. Hillary worked herself up to fuming by the time she reached the kitchen for some much-needed coffee.

"Hey there, book girl," came a familiar, oily voice.

Hillary was so lost in her anger and confusion, she hadn't even noticed Keith was in the kitchen this morning.

"Morning," she replied indifferently as she went about getting a cup for her coffee. Beatrice had the pot set on a timer to brew first thing, every morning. And, as usual, there were fresh bagels from a shop down the street on the counter.

"Looking a little rough there, book girl." His teasing emphasis on the nickname only served to increase her annoyance. "Long night?"

Hillary had no desire to carry on a conversation. All she wanted was to get her breakfast, in peace, so she could go back to her room and be alone. The problem was her mood was written all over her face which only encouraged Keith to continue antagonizing her. All she could do was hurry up with preparing her bagel and coffee. There was normally cut fresh fruit in the refrigerator, but Hillary would skip it this morning. At this point, she was willing to eat her bagel untoasted and dry if it meant getting out this kitchen faster.

"Didn't sleep well," she responded, flatly.

Keith smirked at her. He was leaning against a cabinet, staring at her. His arms folded over his protruding gut. She wondered if he ever changed that stained undershirt he wore. Hillary was halfway across the kitchen from him but could still smell the stink of stale alcohol mixed with body odor.

"Didn't sleep well, huh?" he asked. "Well, there's an easy way to fix that, you know." From the corner of her eye, Hillary saw him nod at her as he unfolded his arms, adjusting himself through his grease stained, sagging jeans.

Hillary felt the adrenaline start to pulse through her. He wasn't just antagonizing her. Hillary was suddenly conscious of the fact that there were no sounds coming from the dining room, where Dr. Immerman and Evelyn usually took their breakfast. It was too early for either of them to be down. Robert didn't take his meals in the house. Where was Beatrice? She tried to calm herself, focusing her attention on preparing the bagel that had just popped up from the toaster. Hillary tried to stop her hands from shaking as she cut off a too big glob of cream cheese from the block Beatrice left on the counter to soften. She scraped it onto the edge of her plate.

"Aww, she's shy," he taunted her.

Hillary could feel her stomach knotting. Was he moving closer? She didn't want to look. Instead, she tried to keep her focus on adding lox and a slice of tomato to her plate. All she had to do was pour her coffee. Hillary told herself she was standing her ground. Trying to control her breathing as she raised her chin, hoping she looked more confident than she felt. With everything else going on, she was not going to let this disgusting puke of a man chase her off from her breakfast.

"What's the matter? Did I embarrass you?" he asked, menacingly.

This time she was sure he was moving closer to her, but she still wouldn't let herself look at him. Hillary could suddenly feel him standing right next to her. The stench of stale liquor and old sweat nearly made her gag. He was close enough that his gut brushed her arm. She instinctively flinched away from him. Keith shifted closer to her.

"Come on," he whispered. "I'm just trying to be friendly."

Hillary couldn't move. Her pulse was pounding in her ears. She had to think. Her mind was jumped to imaging what was about to happen. She had to do something. She thought about screaming but his hand would be over her mouth before anyone would hear her. The butter knife she had been using was too far out of reach. She pressed herself forward into the cabinets in front of her. She couldn't get into the drawer. She didn't know what was in it, even if she could. She felt Keith shift closer to her again.

"You want to be friendly, don't you?" his breath hissed in her ear. She pushed her body forward, tighter against the counter. His gut was still touching her. She couldn't move away.

"Good morning," came a loud voice from the doorway to the dining room. Hillary lifted her eyes to see Dr. Immerman standing there, taking in the scene. "Is everything alright in here?"

Keith immediately backed away. Hillary straightened away from the counter, still tense, not taking her eyes off Dr. Immerman.

"Just saying good morning to my tenants." Keith's tone was casual.

Hillary didn't say anything. She grabbed her plate, the knife, and a napkin. She moved to the other end of the kitchen. Hillary filled the coffee cup she set out before making a swift exit from the kitchen. She'd take her coffee black this morning. She hurried down the hall and up the front stairs, not taking a breath until she closed the door behind her, in her room. She stood there, her plate in one hand, coffee in the other. She closed her eyes, panting from the adrenaline, her heart racing. Hillary squeezed her eyes tighter, trying to calm herself. A large tear escaped from each eye and rolled down her cheek. The sudden knock at her door caused her to tense all over again.

"Hillary, it's Dr. Immerman. Are you alright?" he called.

Hillary relaxed again, taking a few breaths before she could respond. "I'm fine," she managed.

"Are you sure?" he asked in a raised voice.

"Yes, I'm fine," she replied again, her breakfast still in her hands.

"I'd like to talk to you about what happened. Will you open the door? I'll stay out in the hallway." His voice was concerned.

Hillary looked around her room. She placed her breakfast on her desk before opening the door. His face was one of fatherly concern and compassion.

"It's okay," she said avoiding his gaze. "You can come in, if you want to." She moved aside so he could enter her room.

"Are you sure?" he asked. "I can talk to you from here, if you'd rather."

"No, it's alright. You can come in," she responded.

He stepped past her, through the door, glancing around the unkempt room. Her bed was still unmade and there was a pile of laundry on the floor. Papers were strewn across her desk, by the windows and a stack of books sat haphazardly on a small table beside the bed. Dr. Immerman wished he stayed in the hallway.

"Please sit," she said, closing the door.

He pulled the chair out from her desk, turning it around before seating himself. She perched herself on the edge of her unmade bed, not meeting his gaze. He turned to pick up her coffee off the desk and handed it to her.

"Here. Have a sip of this," he urged.

Hillary took a sip of the bitter coffee, easing back further onto the bed and folding up her legs in front of her. Dr. Immerman waited patiently in silence.

"When you're ready, can you tell me what happened?" Dr. Immerman asked her.

"Nothing happened, really," she replied, settling her coffee cup in her hands. "I was getting my breakfast and he was suddenly there. He started teasing me. He just moved next to me when you came in."

"Do you want to file a report? I'll make a statement, if you do," he offered.

Hillary just shook her head. She was humiliated. All she wanted was to be alone. She kept her eyes fixed on the coffee cup in her hands.

"Men get away with things like that if you keep silent," he said. His tone turned less patient.

"I'm fine," she responded. "Nothing happened." Hillary stood up at this. "If you'll excuse me, I'd like to get some work done and eat my breakfast." She moved across the room to the door, opening it. "Thank you for your concern." She didn't look at him.

Dr. Immerman rose from her desk chair. "Alright." He crossed the room to the door. He stopped in front of her. "If you need anything, let me know," he told her before moving back into the hallway.

"Thank you," she said quietly before closing the door.

11

Evelyn was at her breaking point. Midway through the semester and she was ready to fire every intern in the place. None of them could show up on time. One couldn't ever seem to reshelf books in their proper place. It wasn't that complicated of a system! She finally decided to hide in the research room for an hour or so to cool down. She grabbed her notes and a cup of tea before getting comfortable in front of microfiche reader. Some time with the Browns was just what she needed right now.

Evelyn decided to focus her work on births, deaths, and marriages today. She needed to piece together whatever happened in the 1950s. Maybe something in the family's history would hold a clue. She located the marriage announcement for William Brown Senior and his wife. The couple was pictured, unsmiling, in a black and white studio photo. The bride was dressed in a dark colored dress with a high neck and slightly puffed sleeves. Evelyn was surprised the couple wasn't more regally dressed. They certainly had the money and standing for a lavish, society wedding. Evelyn puzzled at this but decided it probably wasn't significant. And given how long ago the couple married, probably had nothing to do with their son's eventual exodus from town. She studied the photo a minute or two more before moving on with her search.

Next, she found a brief wedding announcement that mentioned the daughter of William Brown. It was only a partial record that didn't give many details. Evelyn read it over a few times. William Brown Senior didn't have a daughter. The announcement must be the marriage of William Brown Junior's daughter. There was a date and a mention of the reception being held at the bride's family home. But nothing more. The daughter wasn't even named in the clip. Evelyn jotted down the date of the marriage, which occurred in 1944. She would have to look for another source. William Brown Junior's daughter had been married six or seven years before the Maple Street House was abandoned.

Evelyn sat back, sipping her tea. The young, naïve Miss Brown contracts a marriage with a man who turns out to be a scoundrel. The new son in law soaks the family for their fortune and they leave town in disgrace. New son in law ends up the unlikely heir to a title in Europe. The whole family packs it in to cross the pond where he's to become the Marquess of somewhere no one has ever heard of. Evelyn laughed to herself. None of this was probably what happened but she liked to imagine uncovering something really outlandish when she did her research projects. And today, her musings were much needed. She could feel herself relaxing.

Evelyn scrolled on to an obituary for William Brown Senior. Nothing in it was anything she didn't already know. It was followed by an obituary for William Brown Junior. This was a little more helpful. Mr. Brown Junior died in the early 1970s. So a sudden death of Brown Junior wasn't what caused the family to abandon the house. The source of the article was missing, and the location of his death wasn't mentioned. The obituary gave a brief history of the man. Evelyn noticed that it was really very generic, especially compared to what had been written about his father. Evelyn read back over it a second time. There was no mention of surviving family members. Evelyn scrolled to the next page, expecting to find the obituary continued. Instead it was an announcement of another kind. Evelyn scrolled back without reading it.

Evelyn wondered at this. William Brown Junior is laid to rest with a very generic published eulogy and no mention of surviving family members. Instinct told her this was something she needed to make note of. This man was the head of a wealthy, well-respected family and this was all that was written about him at the time of his death. It just didn't make sense. But then Evelyn studied the date again. He died around twenty years after the Maple Street house was abandoned. Nothing about this made any sense.

The sound of footsteps entering the research room caught Evelyn's attention. This time of day wasn't popular with students on campus. Most of them didn't use this room anyway. Evelyn glanced up in the direction of the sound. Her look of annoyance at the interruption stopped her intern, Nina, in her tracks.

"Oh gosh," she stammered. "I'm so sorry Ms. Berke. I can come back later." Nina made a hasty retreat from the room.

Evelyn let out a heavy sigh before turning back to her research. She should really be getting back to work. Evelyn shrugged to herself. The fire alarm would alert her if her interns did anything else they weren't supposed to. She made a few more notes about Brown Junior's obituary before she scrolled on to the next record.

This was something new. It was an article about the christening of a grandchild. One that was celebrated in high style, judging by the picture. A large group was gathered in what must be the gardens at the Maple Street house. They were beautiful. A baby lay in the arms of a young mother, in an elegant christening gown, that draped over the young woman's lap. Evelyn studied the picture. The couple with the baby wasn't William Brown Junior and his wife. So, this baby wasn't the same little girl with the extravagant doll she found in photos earlier. Evelyn made some notes of dates before she started reading. William Brown and his wife were pleased to announce the christening of their grandson. There was a smudge in the page where the baby's name was mentioned but he'd been born in 1945. Evelyn went back to the photo, zooming in on the mother's face. The photo quality was good for the time period. The young woman's eyes were the same as the little girl in earlier photos. This was William Brown Junior's daughter, holding her baby son. Her face was serene. Evelyn took a closer look at the other people around her. There were young men seated on either side of her. One was likely the child's father, the other probably the godfather.

Evelyn smiled at the photo. The young woman looked so happy. She reviewed her notes. So the daughter had been married around 1944 and welcomed a baby boy a year later. But this was all several years before the house was abandoned. Evelyn sat back and studied the picture. There was nothing in the article naming the other people in the photo. She picked out William Brown and his wife, the proud grandparents. There was another woman who looked to be a similar age to the Browns. Probably a paternal grandmother. She could also be an aunt.

Evelyn felt frustrated. She'd been working on this project long enough that, by now, she should have at least some clue about what happened in the 1950s. But she felt no closer to it than she had been the first day of her research. There had to be something. Evelyn decided to peek at just one more record before she went back to work. She scrolled a little further, angrily, before she gave up. This was a mystery she wasn't going to solve today.

12

The coffee shop where Hillary went to hear the poetry reading had become her second home. One might argue it was her first home considering how much more time she was spending there than at Maple Street. She felt uncomfortable there, even with the door locked. She'd stopped taking breakfast in the mornings. Instead coming to the coffee shop for a latte. She had been skipping dinners in the evening. Hillary couldn't bring herself to face Dr. Immerman. Beatrice had been leaving trays outside her door in the evenings. Usually with just a sandwich and something to drink. Hillary assumed Beatrice probably wasn't supposed to be doing that. She didn't venture out of her room at night anymore.

Hillary was looking for other apartments. There wasn't much available in the middle of the term, in such a small town. And what was out there was either too expensive or too far from campus. She met with a trio of girls who were looking for another roommate. But the place had been a two-bedroom apartment, not much bigger than her entire room on Maple Street, and she would be sharing a room with another girl.

The group were friends since middle school. They'd gone to summer camp together. It was like they spoke their own language that Hillary was never going to be able to learn. And it made her miss Rachel all the more. They invited her to move in after the meeting, but Hillary declined.

Hillary decided to pick up some hours at the coffee shop. She really didn't have time to work if she was going to stay on track at school. But she was spending all her time there anyway and the extra funds would help. Who needs sleep anyway, she'd told herself, on getting up at five after working until after midnight for an acoustic night, her first week. She was covering a morning shift for a co-worker before her afternoon class when Dr. Immerman stopped in.

"There you are," he greeted her. "Are you living here now?" Hillary could never quite tell if he was joking or not.

"I picked up some hours to help with expenses," she answered, handing him his change.

"You haven't been taking your evening meals. I was starting to worry," he explained.

"Beatrice brings my dinner on a tray. I haven't felt much like coming down lately. And I've been really busy," she responded.

"Right," he said flatly. "I think you've been avoiding everyone else in the house because you're embarrassed about what happened the other morning."

She stood behind the counter, motionless. She hadn't expected such a blunt remark but then look who she was talking to.

"I didn't tell anyone what happened," he went on. "If you don't want to talk about it, that's entirely your own affair."

If Hillary wasn't mistaken, there was a note of compassion in his voice. Not something she expected from the man who hardly acknowledged her existence.

"Keith doesn't come around during evening meals. I hope you'll rejoin us soon," he said. Then after a pause, "If for no other reason than I won't have to make conversation with Ms. Berke." With this, he turned from the counter and took a seat at small table near the front window.

Hillary went back to cleaning up from the morning rush. As she was washing smoothie out of blenders and refilling supplies behind the counter, she mused at the slip of Dr. Immerman's mask. Hillary learned not to disturb him during his pre-dinner reading in the living room. And he rarely joined in conversation at dinner. But for just a few minutes, he had been concerned about her. Maybe she had misjudged him. She glanced toward the table where he was sitting. He was reading a newspaper while sipping his coffee.

Hillary picked up a bottle of cleaner and a cloth to wipe down tables. The place finally cleared out and she had time to bus the tables. She made her way around the seating area, picking up discarded trash and empty cups. As she worked on the table next to Dr. Immerman's, he looked up from his paper.

"You're a Fine Arts student, aren't you?" he asked.

"Yes, that's right," she responded taking a break from wiping the table and stepping closer to him.

"Poet or painter?" he asked. Hillary smiled.

"Writer. Aspiring historical fiction author," she answered, matching his cadence.

"What time period," he asked.

"Umm, I haven't really specialized at this point." She felt a little silly giving that answer but it was the truth.

"Hmm, really," he replied, picking up his paper again.

Hillary went back to wiping the table next to him, assuming she had been dismissed. He lowered his paper again.

"You spend a lot of time at the library. What are you researching?" he asked.

"I've been working on some other things," she said quickly. "I haven't really been researching."

"An historical fiction writer who doesn't do research," he remarked. "Interesting."

Hillary didn't know quite what to say to this. She was working on pieces for her portfolio, but they had been primarily pieces to meet her poetry requirements. She never liked poetry much but just lately she'd been feeling motivated to write more verse. Her idealized notions of Robert were inspiring her to the point of distraction. She got a lecture from her advisor at their last meeting that she needed to try a different theme to round out her portfolio. Her advisor also warned her the sentimental mush she'd been writing wasn't worth reading.

Hillary's thoughts turned to Robert. She hadn't seen him since she had been spending what little time she was spending at the house, locked in her room. But by now, her neighbors must have run into him.

"Dr. Immerman, I was wondering if you have had a chance to meet Robert yet?" she asked.

Dr. Immerman had gone back to reading his paper and didn't immediately look up when she posed the question. She was about to repeat herself when he lowered his paper and studied her a minute.

"Who?" he asked.

"Robert. He's in the room next to the bathroom, across the hall from Evelyn," she explained.

"The room next to the bathroom?" he questioned her.

"Yes, that's right. He moved in shortly before I did. Maybe a few months before," she answered.

"I can't say that I have ever seen anyone come or go from that room. I had no idea it was rented. Does this young man of yours keep odd hours?" he asked. Hillary blushed at hearing Robert called her young man.

"He's not my young man," she replied a little too quickly. "You must be right. He must just keep odd hours. I ran into him in the hallway, late one night, when I was getting something from the kitchen."

"I'm sorry. I haven't had the pleasure of meeting this young man you say isn't yours," his lips turned up in a slight, teasing smile.

Hillary's embarrassment rose further at his facial expression. She glanced around nervously, looking for a way out of this conversation. She shouldn't have even brought it up. She was trying to think of something that needed her attention when the bell above the door chimed. Customers came in through the front door.

"Excuse me," she muttered quickly, turning to go back behind the counter.

Dr. Immerman turned back to his paper, shaking his head with a smile.

13

Hillary tucked her scarf a little closer around her neck against the chill. She was on her way back to Maple Street after finishing a shift at the coffee shop. Her pace was slower than usual and her stomach was in knots. Her rent was due. She would have to see Keith. For reasons surpassing her understanding, Keith insisted on his tenants turning in their rent, in person. As far as she was concerned, there was no reason a drop box couldn't be installed somewhere so they could deposit it without having to interact with him. She hadn't seen him since the morning she ran into him in the kitchen. She was still uneasy being around the house and was always sure to put the door chain on, when she was home. She went back to taking her evening meals with Evelyn and Dr. Immerman. She still refused to venture out of her room at night. But there was no avoiding him this time. Rent not delivered in person was considered not received.

Hillary knew this time of day Evelyn would still be at the library. Dr. Immerman was either in class or keeping office hours, which meant he wouldn't be around the house either.

She hadn't seen Robert in ages. But Beatrice would likely be in the kitchen, preparing their evening meal. Hillary also hoped Dottie would be around. She hadn't seen her again since their encounter in the kitchen. If Tommy was in school somewhere, he should have come home by now too. Provided he wasn't in some sort of after school lesson or activity. Dottie could be out running errands too. But she seemed to be determined to have dinner on the table by a certain hour. Hillary's best hope at not being alone with Keith was Dottie being home, preparing his dinner.

She finally pressed herself into a faster pace. It was cold out this afternoon and she wanted to get out of the weather. As she came in, she heard Beatrice in the kitchen.

"Hi Beatrice," Hillary greeted her, stepping into the kitchen.

"Hello, dear," Beatrice replied. "Meatloaf tonight."

"Sounds great. I'm just going to pop down to the basement to make my rent payment. Do you know if Keith is in?" Hillary hoped Beatrice would say he was out. That way she could put it off a little longer.

"I think I heard him down there. He should be in," said Beatrice, stirring something on the stove.

"Okay, thank you," Hillary said turning to go down the stairs. She stood in the doorway a minute, gathering her courage. This was only going to take a second. Beatrice was just at the top of the stairs. She made sure the door stayed open and she started down.

About halfway down the stairs, Hillary registered sounds of an argument coming from the basement.

"No, please," pleaded a woman. "Please don't do that. I'll do better. I promise."

Hillary stopped.

"Oh, you'll do better, will you?! You'll do better. Seems like you're always going to do better," an angry male voice yelled. "Why can't you just do it right to begin with? Why can't you do anything right?"

There was silence.

"I'm sorry," sobbed the woman.

"You're sorry? Come here. I'll make you sorry," the male voice was in a rage. Something crashed. The woman screamed. "Shut up," barked the male. The sound of a hand delivering a blow followed. The woman cried out.

Hillary couldn't move.

"I work my ass off all day long. And all I ask is a clean house and a decent dinner. Is that too goddamn much to ask?" the male yelled. "Is it?!"

The female's response was short but too soft to make out.

"No, it shouldn't be. But look around. This place looks like a dump. And whatever the hell you call that slop smells like it's burnt. What the hell do you even do around here all day?"

"I'll start over. I can make it right. Just give me a few minutes. I'll make you a nice meal," the crying female pleaded. "Please don't."

The male's voice responded but it was too low for Hillary to make out what he was saying.

"Do I make myself clear," the male finally yelled.

"Yes," the female replied. "I promise. I can do better."

"You damn well better. Or you know what's going to happen," the male barked. "Useless, you're goddamn useless. I don't know why I keep you around here."

The argument seemed to have ended. Hillary remained frozen on the stairs.

"Making me eat this damn slop," the male started again. "Here, here's what I think of this goddamn slop."

"No, please. Don't do that," the female called in alarm before something heavy crashed.

"Now clean this shit up and make me something decent to eat," the male shouted. "Get to it, woman! You're so damn slow. And quit that damn crying. I've heard enough."

All was quiet again. Hillary didn't know what to do. She thought about turning around and going back to her room.

She could pay her rent late this month. But how could she do that to that sweet woman after what she just heard? She was certain Keith had hit Dottie. But she couldn't just confront him. What was she going to do? If she knocked on the door now, he would know she heard. That she knew what he did to his wife. But she doubted he would care if he realized she knew or that it would change anything. Hillary gathered herself and continued down the stairs. At least Dottie would know she heard. That Hillary knew what her brute of a husband was doing to her in this dingy basement. There had to be some way Hillary could help. But she couldn't do it by herself.

As Hillary reached the door to knock, she heard the male voice again, "Don't you have that shit cleaned up yet?! And I thought I told you quit your damn crying!"

Hillary knocked hard. She heard Keith's sluggish, heavy, shuffling steps approaching and the lock unbolting.

"What?" Keith demanded as he opened the door.

"Umm, I'm making my rent payment," Hillary stammered.

He was more disheveled looking than usual, leaning heavily on the door frame. All was quiet in the apartment behind him. She wondered where Tommy was. Did he have a hiding spot when his father acted like this? Dottie must have realized Hillary heard the argument. She hoped Dottie wasn't embarrassed. Maybe Dottie knowing that Hillary knew how Keith treated her would give her hope.

"So you gonna stand here all night or you gonna give me your rent?" Keith demanded.

"Oh, sorry. I just," she trailed off as she reached into her bag, digging for the envelope with the payment.

Her hands fumbled. She suddenly realized she was shaking. Keith didn't move. He just glared at her from the doorway. Finally, she found the envelope, holding it out to him. He snatched it quickly from her hand and closed the door without another word. She heard the lock bolt snap back into place. Hillary waited. She heard Keith's steps shuffle away from the door but there was no other sound. She turned and went back up the stairs.

14

Evelyn pulled her fleece throw over her lap as she settled into the oversized chair in her room to go back over her notes. She just came home for having coffee with the woman from the historical society. The coffee date hadn't been as enlightening as Evelyn hoped. Time had certainly clouded the woman's memory. She moved out of the area, with her husband, shortly after they married. She moved back eventually but it was about ten years after the Browns left. By then, it had become something no one discussed anymore.

The woman had been more interested in regaling Evelyn with tales of attending a handful of dances with Billy, as she insisted on calling him, back when they were young. But this was long before William Junior married, had a child, and inherited the Maple Street house. She had apparently been the envy of every young woman of society back then. She hoped they would eventually marry. Unfortunately, Billy's parents had other plans for him. They arranged a marriage with the daughter of a family even wealthier than the

Browns. She had been heartbroken at reading the news of their engagement in the paper. Billy apparently neglected to mention he was involved in another courtship. Interesting as this period soap opera was, it was of no help to Evelyn.

Evelyn tried to move the conversation toward the more recent past. Maybe this woman tried to look up her old beau when she moved back to the area. But she hadn't. Just before Evelyn was going to cut off their meeting, the woman suddenly remembered a line in a letter, from her sister, about the family taking in a boarder. It had been sometime around 1950. She seemed to think it had something to do with the Korean conflict. Evelyn wrote this down, but the woman didn't remember any other details. Evelyn asked about meeting the woman's sister. Unfortunately, she passed away a few years ago.

Evelyn picked up her laptop and connected to the college's research network. If this woman's sister knew about the Browns taking in a boarder, was it possible there had been an article about it? Evelyn wondered at a connection between the boarder and the family leaving town. When she'd heard of William Junior's financially advantageous marriage, she had all but eliminated the possibility of financial ruin. There was just no way that was the case. But now, she wondered. Why would the family take in a boarder? If the woman from the historical society was right, they took this person in within a year of when the house had been abandoned. There had to be a connection.

Evelyn pulled up the archives search form. She wasn't sure where to begin looking for something like this. Her first few attempts at search terms didn't yield any results. Her frustration was starting to grow. She finally found the clue she'd been looking for. Only to be foiled by an elderly woman with no curiosity over what happened to an old beau who dropped her for a bride with a bigger purse. Evelyn drummed her fingers against her keyboard. There had to be something out there about this. It was the Brown family. At one time, the local papers wrote about practically everything this family did. Their grandson's birth had been front page news. How was it possible that this was the one thing none of the papers bothered to cover?

She looked back over her notes. The woman from the historical society thought the Brown family's boarder had some connection to the Korean conflict. She typed in Brown and war effort. She let out a long sigh as she smiled. There it was. The article she had been looking for. She wondered how it hadn't come up with her other search terms. She clicked the article heading to load the page.

Evelyn set her laptop aside as the article loaded. This breakthrough called for a celebratory cup of tea. Evelyn tossed her fleece throw aside and went down to the kitchen. It was late afternoon and Beatrice was busy in the kitchen.

"Is the kettle hot?" she asked, standing in the doorway, not wanting to get in Beatrice's way. She typically avoided the kitchen at this hour.

"Yes, dear. Help yourself. I'd get it for you but I'm working on a shepherd's pie for tonight and I'm running late," Beatrice answered.

"No problem. Just didn't want to get in your way. I've had a breakthrough in my research project and decided to celebrate with tea," Evelyn explained.

"Good for you, dear," Beatrice answered, not looking up from her chopping. Evelyn tried talking to Beatrice about her work in the past. Beatrice never took much interest in it.

Evelyn prepared her tea and made her way back upstairs. She settled back into her chair with her laptop. The article made William Junior sound righteously benevolent. Evelyn expected nothing less when it came to coverage of this family. Everything they did was utterly celebrated. The Browns, in an effort to support wounded returning soldiers, opened their home to a Captain, recently returned from the conflict in Korea. The article included a photo of William Junior, his wife, and an attractive looking young man in an army uniform. The photo was taken on the front porch of the Maple Street house. Evelyn noted the Browns' daughter was not present. The article went on and on about the Browns' various efforts to support the cause. It ended with a call to action for others to step up and do their part.

Evelyn scrolled back to the photo. The caption named the Browns. There was no mention of the young Captain's name. He wasn't named in the article either. Whatever his injuries had been, they weren't obvious in the photo. The young man's expression was very serious.

"Okay, Captain," Evelyn said to the photo. "What is your name? And what was your part in the Browns leaving Maple Street?"

Evelyn downloaded a copy of the photo. Maybe she would get lucky with an image search. She'd found people that way before. Evelyn was just about to run the photo when she glanced at the clock. Her research would have to wait. It was time to head down to dinner.

15

Hillary was still a little shaken from the argument she heard coming from Keith's apartment. She looked again for another apartment but there were no new postings. Even the extra money she was making, working at the coffee shop, didn't make a difference. She was stuck. There hadn't been an opportunity to tell Dr. Immerman or Evelyn about it. She wondered if they heard Keith before. Neither of them seemed to have any interest in him. Dr. Immerman didn't even know Keith's wife. Beatrice had to be aware of what was going on. She could easily hear it from the kitchen. Were these people really that indifferent?

Hillary's obsessing was keeping her from getting any work done on her portfolio. She got up early to try to get some writing done. But so far, she hadn't written a word. Hillary glanced at the clock. It should be a safe hour to finally go downstairs for breakfast. She heard Dr. Immerman leave his room a few minutes ago.

Hillary unbolted the lock on her door and went out into the hallway. Her head was swimming with what to do about Keith's treatment of his wife. She pulled her sweater a little tighter. The hallway was oddly cold this morning.

"Good morning," said Robert, standing outside his door. She hadn't even seen him.

"Hi," she answered with a slight smile. She planned to walk right by if she ran into him again. She would heed Rachel's advice and move on.

"Where are you off to in such a hurry this morning?" he asked.

Hillary was confused. The other times she ran into him, Robert didn't seem to take any interest in her. She stopped walking and turned to him.

"I was just heading downstairs to get breakfast," she answered.

"Most important meal of the day," he responded with a big smile. She smiled at the cliché. It was amazing how much more relaxed she felt. Now that she lost interest in him, that is.

"I haven't seen you for a while," she remarked. See, conversations weren't so hard.

"I have been away," he answered.

That explained it. No wonder no one else in the house had seen him. And why he hadn't answered the door when she tried to invite him to the poetry reading. And why she hadn't seen him in several weeks. He was out of town. Just when she thought she'd gotten over the idea of him, she was suddenly right back in it. Hillary shifted her weight, feeling the awkwardness starting to rise up again.

"You look lovely this morning, Miss Hillary," he remarked.

Wait, was he flirting with her? Hillary couldn't believe it. Maybe, after all, there was something here. She smiled broadly at his compliment.

"Thank you," she answered. Before she could overthink, she heard herself say, "I was wondering if you might be interested in going out some time. There's an acoustic night at the coffee shop, where I work, this Tuesday. I have the night off. We could go together."

Robert's charismatic smile started to fade, taking Hillary's optimism with it. She started mentally kicking herself. She jumped in too quickly. She should have talked a little more. Or maybe she should have waited for him to ask her first. He probably didn't like her being so forward. She imagined he was very traditional. She could have offered him her number first. That seemed a little unnecessary, since she lived right down the hall. Either way, whatever answer she was about to get, it was going to be a no.

"I'm sorry, Hillary. You seem like a very nice girl, but I can't," Robert responded.

"If Tuesday doesn't work, we could go another time. Or if you're not into acoustic nights, we could do something else." Hillary could hear the desperation in her voice, but she couldn't stop herself.

"No, it's not that. I'm afraid it's a complicated situation," Robert started to explain.

"Good morning," called Evelyn, coming up the back stairs and cutting him off.

Hillary turned her head toward Evelyn. When she looked back, Robert was gone. Hillary was confused at how he could have gone back into his room without her seeing him go. Or hearing the door latch. She was staring at the door as Evelyn got closer.

"Hillary. Are you okay?" Evelyn asked.

"Umm, yeah. I'm fine," Hillary replied, still not looking away from the door.

"Are you sure? You don't seem yourself," Evelyn said. Hillary finally looked away from the door.

"I'm sorry. I was just talking to Robert, but he went back into his room when you came up the stairs," Hillary explained. Evelyn's brow knitted in confusion.

"There's someone renting that room?" she asked.

"Yes. He said he was away for a while. That's why you didn't hear anyone coming or going from the room," Hillary explained.

"Oh," said Evelyn. Her brow was still knitted as she studied the door. "I'm glad I ran into you actually. I've had a breakthrough in my research about the house. I'm really excited about it."

"Really," Hillary responded politely.

Evelyn launched into an explanation of her research. Something about the house being abandoned and a coffee with an elderly woman who knew the previous owners. An article about a young man who was wounded in the Korean conflict. Evelyn was talking a mile a minute, obviously excited. Hillary wasn't listening to a word. Her focus turned back to Robert's door as Evelyn continued on.

She finally started to make a little progress with him. She had been confident and not awkward. Then it had all gone wrong. Robert turned down her invitation to go out on a date. But before he could explain why, he disappeared. It was like he vanished into thin air when Evelyn came up the stairs. She got her hopes up again only to be disappointed. Finally, she couldn't take Evelyn babbling on about her work anymore.

"I'm sorry," she interrupted Evelyn. "I was just on my way downstairs for breakfast so I can get back to work. Will you excuse me?"

Hillary brushed past her and hurried down the back stairs without another word. Evelyn just shrugged and went into her room. Hillary decided on coffee and some fruit over yogurt for breakfast today. She didn't want to spend time waiting for a bagel to toast. Hillary was scooping yogurt into a bowl when she heard the sound of a glass breaking. It was coming from the basement. Hillary froze. She could hear the sound of a muffled voice yelling, followed by a softer, pleading female. Then a thud. Hillary closed her eyes. She had no reason to go down to Keith's apartment, but she couldn't stand by and let this go on. It was wrong. But she couldn't just go storming down there by herself. It wasn't like she could overpower Keith, if she needed to. He was at least twice her size. She was debating what she could safely do, as the sounds of the fight continued on, when Beatrice came back into the kitchen, from the dining room.

"Good morning, dear," she greeted Hillary.

"Good morning," Hillary responded nervously, adding fruit to her bowl.

Another clatter came from the basement. Beatrice crossed the kitchen to the basement door, closing it. Hillary watched in shock.

"That nephew of mine really needs to exercise his demons," Beatrice remarked, moving to a cabinet to retrieve something.

"Keith is your nephew?" Hillary asked. She hadn't realized this.

"Yes, dear. My sister's son," Beatrice answered. "He's always had his issues. It caught up to him though."

"Really?" Hillary asked, hoping if she kept her remarks short Beatrice would keep talking.

"He spent a little time away after he got himself into some trouble," she explained. "That was a long time ago now, but he's never been the same."

"Some time away?" Hillary asked.

"Prison, dear," Beatrice responded. That's what Hillary thought she'd meant. Keith had done time. "When he came back, his mother had died. I decided to help him out. I owed my sister that much. I swear she died of a broken heart when he went away. I gave him some money to get him back on his feet. He bought this house. Had big plans to fix it up and sell it but he's always been foolish with money. When he decided to take in tenants, I moved in to help him out."

Hillary stood awkwardly. Her breakfast was ready. She really needed to get back upstairs and get to work. She felt like she should say something, but she wasn't sure what.

"Listen to me, carrying on. You probably have things to do. Go on now," Beatrice said.

Hillary smiled at her gently. It was like Beatrice read her mind.

"Thank you, Beatrice," Hillary said politely, raising her coffee and bowl of yogurt.

"You're welcome, dear," she replied, smiling at Hillary's gratitude. Hillary turned and headed back to her room.

16

Hillary was walking on air. Rachel was finally coming for a visit! Three whole days with her best friend. She had been feeling so out of sorts with Robert giving her the brush off and that thing with Keith, at breakfast. Hearing Keith's raging temper at his poor wife. She was so far off track with her portfolio, Hillary wasn't sure she would ever get caught up. But none of that mattered because she was rushing out the door to meet Rachel's train from the airport. Hillary was so distracted, she nearly ran directly into Dottie as she rushed toward the door, in the kitchen.

"Oh my gosh," Hillary exclaimed, stopping short. "I am so sorry!" Dottie's expression was equally startled.

"He's going to be home any minute," she babbled, "I have to make sure the house is spotless. I don't have much time."

Hillary failed to notice little Tommy, standing at his mother's side. Dottie had him by the hand. He wore the same button-down shirt, neatly tucked into his pants, he wore when she met them before. His brown lace up shoes looked worn. He smiled up at her, grinning wide, so all his teeth were visible. Hillary looked back at Dottie and realized she was also wearing the same dress. Her hair neatly sculpted in the same style. She was stunningly beautiful.

"Good morning, Tommy," she greeted him. He didn't reply. "Are you alright, Dottie? Is there something I can do to help you?"

"Oh no, everything is fine," she replied hastily, trying to smile. There was a sadness in her face. "I just really need to get the house cleaned up before he gets home. He does like a clean house."

"Are you sure there isn't someone I could call, to help you? A family member or a friend," Hillary offered.

"Of course not. Everything is perfectly well," Dottie's words were rushed. "Come along now Tommy. Lots to do."

Hillary caught a chill as Dottie turned on her kitten heel, the skirt of her dress swishing about her legs with the movement. She led Tommy along toward the basement stairs. He looked back at Hillary, a little nervously.

"Please don't trouble yourself," Dottie told Hillary, pausing at the top of the basement stairs. With that, she started down. Her feet so light on the stairs, Hillary realized she didn't hear a single clack from Dottie's heels.

Hillary stood a minute longer in the kitchen, hoping Dottie would come back up the stairs. Or maybe Tommy would break free from his mother's grasp and come running back. Hillary felt helpless. She glanced at her phone for the time. Realizing she was going to be late, she rushed out the door to her car to meet Rachel.

✳✳✳

Hillary made it to the station just as Rachel's train pulled in. They'd hugged on the platform for what seemed like forever. They had a lot of catching up to do.

"Okay so what's the latest with this guy in your building? You haven't said much about him lately," Rachel asked on the drive back to Maple Street.

"Not much to tell, really," Hillary started. "I ran into him last week, on my way down to breakfast."

"And?" Rachel prompted.

"And I ran into him," Hillary responded. "I asked him if he wanted to go out some time. He shot me down but before I could find out why, it was like he disappeared."

"What do you mean he disappeared?" Rachel asked.

"One minute he was turning down my invitation to go to an acoustic night. Then my other neighbor, Evelyn, came up the stairs. When I turned back to him, he was just gone. Like he vanished. I didn't even hear his door close. And I was standing right in front of it."

"Okay, that's just weird," Rachel responded. "I mean, who does that?!"

"I know," Hillary said.

"What did he say? When you asked him to go out? We'll get to why you thought inviting him to an acoustic night at a coffeehouse was a good idea in a minute. I don't know how you can stand those. It's like low budget karaoke but worse."

Hillary laughed. "I thought it was a casual, no pressure thing to do. And some of the people I've heard there are really good."

"Yeah, okay. Some chick named Fern strumming her guitar and singing weird, breathy songs, like it's the 70s or something. Nothing about that is good," Rachel shot back.

"Okay, okay," Hillary laughed, "so it wasn't a perfect plan. But it was the first thing I thought of. And I should get serious points for even asking him in the first place."

"Fine, I'll give you that. But we seriously need to work on your game. Have I taught you nothing?!" Rachel teased.

"Whatever," Hillary rolled her eyes. "Anyway, he said he couldn't and that it was complicated."

"It's complicated?! What exactly is complicated? His wife and kids back in Toledo?" Rachel asked.

"Like I said, I never got the chance to ask. Evelyn came up the stairs and he was just gone," Hillary said. "Do you think that's it? That he's married?"

"I don't know," Rachel responded. "Did you do a ring check?"

Hillary scrunched up her face.

"Hil, you didn't do a ring check?!" Rachel scolded.

"I just forget that. I forget that we're old enough that people are married now," Hillary said, trying to justify the lapse. "Speaking of ring checks, how are things with you and Miguel?"

"Who?" Rachel asked as though she never heard of him.

"Miguel. The veterinarian who was teaching you Spanish," Hillary responded.

"Oh right, yeah, that didn't work out," Rachel said as if it were nothing.

"And the new one's name is?" Hillary asked, sarcastically.

"I'm between at the moment. I'm trying a cooling off period," Rachel replied, trying to make her voice sound posh.

"Wow, that's not like you," Hillary laughed.

"I know. Trying something new," Rachel said, breezily. "What else is going on around here?" They reached the house and were unloading Rachel's bags from the car. She was not a light traveler.

"Umm, well Evelyn has been working on some kind of research project about the house. When Robert pulled his vanishing act, she started going on about the family taking in boarders or something. She seems to think something happened to the family that used to own the house or something. And apparently finding an article about some guy, who was in the army, boarding here was the key to figuring it out. I wasn't really listening, to be honest."

"Well she sounds fascinating," Rachel replied drolly. Hillary laughed.

"She's actually a really interesting person and she's been really nice to me," Hillary replied. "You'll meet her at dinner later."

"Okay. And there's some other professor across the hall from you. What's his deal?" Rachel asked.

"Umm, at first I really didn't like him. He's pretty uptight. But he kind of saved me a while ago," Hillary said, trying to keep her tone casual. They reached Hillary's door. She had her back to Rachel as she was unlocking the door.

"Wait, what?!" Rachel asked.

"It's not that big of a deal," Hillary started, moving aside to let Rachel into her room. "I was getting my breakfast and my creepy landlord started giving me some grief. Dr. Immerman came in and interrupted him. It's fine."

"Giving you some grief? What does that mean?" Rachel demanded.

"It was nothing. Seriously. He started teasing me and he got a little too close. But nothing happened."

"You call that nothing?" Rachel asked, raising her eyebrows.

"Rachel, seriously," Hillary responded. "It was no big deal. But the guy is a serious creeper. Turns out our housekeeper is his aunt. I've met his wife a couple of times. She is beautiful and his little boy is so sweet but he's a complete pig. I feel really bad for her."

Hillary decided it was best to leave out a few details, for the time being.

17

Evelyn woke up too early. Hillary had a friend staying, which had Evelyn worried they would be excessively noisy. They hadn't been, at all. But Evelyn so convinced herself she would need to ask them to keep it down at some point during the night, she'd been unable to get to sleep. She'd given up on sleep and been out the door before even Beatrice was up. She came into the library to continue her work on identifying the Captain who lived with the Brown family.

Evelyn settled in the research room with a fresh cup of coffee. She narrowed her search for the three years just prior to the house being transferred to the bank. There had to be something else out there on the mystery Captain. Her first few search attempts didn't yield anything other than the article she'd already found. Finally, one result caught her attention. It was a wedding announcement for the Browns' daughter.

"Here we go," Evelyn said quietly to herself. "I bet the daughter married the Captain."

Evelyn was getting impatient as the article loaded slowly. She sipped her coffee as her agitation grew. As the article finished loading, Evelyn paused, her coffee cup suspended in midair. The Brown's daughter couldn't have married the Captain. He came to live with the family in 1950. Miss Brown married in 1944 and her son was christened in 1945. Unless Miss Brown's first husband passed away unexpectedly, it was highly unlikely this announcement was for a marriage between Miss Brown and the mystery Captain. And a family like this wouldn't announce her second marriage in a big society announcement. This article wasn't likely what she was looking for. Evelyn's face drooped in disappointment.

The article detailed a perfect springtime wedding. The ceremony had been conducted in the local chapel. The reception was hosted at the bride's home. And as was the custom of the time, the gifts the couple received were enumerated in the article. Evelyn mused at the old-fashioned tradition. Imagine couples today listing off their gifts in their wedding announcement for all the world to see. Although, in the age of social media, one could argue the tradition had come back.

Evelyn enlarged the wedding photo, published with the article. The party was again posed in the gardens of the Maple Street house. They really had been very pretty, when they were still being maintained. The bride's dark hair was set in lovely, softly sculpted curls, framing her glowing face. Her dress in the simple, yet elegant, style of the time period.

There were the parents of the bride, looking stoic. William Junior almost looked pained in the photo. Evelyn continued scanning the faces. She had to stifle a laugh when her eyes landed on the groom.

He looked disheveled, like he'd been involved in some sort of brawl just before the ceremony. His coat was visibly wrinkled, and his tie was askew. His hair looked mussed. Comparing him to his fresh-faced bride, he looked considerably older than her. This was not the clean cut looking young man Evelyn would have expected to be standing beside Miss Brown. Evelyn studied the faces of the people positioned nearest the groom. There was an elderly couple nearest him. By their place in the photo, Evelyn assumed these were the groom's parents. But they looked old enough to be the bride's grandparents. It was easy to see where the groom got his unkempt appearance from. The groom's father also looked rumpled, like he'd slept in his suit.

Evelyn jotted down some details about the groom and his family from the article. She suddenly started to wonder if she had been wrong about the Captain. Maybe he wasn't the key to this story. Maybe the key was this, evidently, disagreeable marriage between the Browns' daughter and this rather uncouth groom. She wasn't ready to give up on her theory about the Captain just yet. But for now, she needed more details about this union. Evelyn was just about to hit search on a new query when her phone started buzzing on the table. The noise of her phone rattling on the tabletop startled her.

Evelyn fumbled as she picked up her phone. It was the woman from the historical society.

Evelyn checked the clock as she picked up the call. Who called this early?

"I found something I think you might be interested in," the woman explained after excusing herself for calling so early. Evelyn was impressed she noticed.

The woman went on about how her sister had once been in charge of the historical society's archives, but the boxes were brought to her house when her sister passed away. They sat in an unused room forever since. But she started going through them, after their coffee. Just this morning, she ran across something Evelyn might find useful. Evelyn started to get impatient with the woman's longwinded lead up to what it was she found. And why it was so important that the woman felt the need to call so early? Not that it mattered. She'd been in the library for over an hour already, but that wasn't the point.

"At first, I didn't think there was anything important in the boxes. Mostly some old ledgers I suppose someone might be interested in. One box had some loose documents. I pulled a stack of them out. And they were covering some family photos. I was pulling them out and that's when I found them," the woman explained.

To Evelyn's annoyance, the woman went on explaining, in painful detail, the cover of each of the small notebooks she found at the bottom of the box. There were six of them in total. The woman hadn't thought much of them until the monogram on the cover of each of them caught her attention. So she finally opened one up.

Evelyn nearly dropped her phone when the woman finally explained what she had found. They were Miss Brown's old diaries.

The woman said she was heading to the coffee shop near campus and could meet Evelyn there in twenty minutes. Evelyn had plenty of time before her real day started at the library. And even if she didn't, she really didn't care about being late. She had to get her hands on those diaries. Evelyn rushed to end the call. She tossed her phone into her bag and raced out of the library, not bothering to turn out the lights.

18

"Ugh," Rachel groaned, pulling her jacket tighter around her neck against the cold, late fall wind. "How do you even live here?" Hillary smirked.

"Come on," she laughed, "it's not that bad." She'd opted for a blanket scarf with her wool jacket that morning.

There was a hint of winter in the air already. Hillary was used to the brisk air. Just a few months in the endless summer of Arizona seemed to have softened Rachel up. They walked to the Hillel center for morning services. Hillary was surprised Rachel wanted to go. She had never been very observant. Her mother insisted Rachel attend major holidays and she had never gone when they were at college together. Hillary tried to observe *Shabbat* in their room a few times, but Rachel showed no interest in it.

"There were some seriously cute guys at *kiddush* this morning. You should go more often," Rachel suggested. Hillary laughed.

"I guess," Hillary said. "I like the Rabbi and some of the other girls are nice. I don't exactly go to services for the scenery. I leave that to you." Hillary's hands were tucked in the pockets of her coat, but she nudged Rachel's arm with her elbow. They laughed together. So much for Rachel's cooling off period.

"If you're secretly hoping Robert is going to magically turn up there one *Shabbat*, it's not going to happen," Rachel said. It was an out of the blue remark.

Hillary avoided talking about him since their ride back from the train station. But secretly she'd hoped they would run into him. She wanted Rachel to meet him. Maybe then she would get it. If she could just meet Robert, Rachel would finally see what Hillary saw. Logically, Hillary knew she should move on. If she was really looking to date, Rachel was right. She was better off meeting someone over *kiddush* than hanging her hopes on the mysterious stranger down the hall. The one who wouldn't give her the time of day and told her it was complicated when she asked him out. But her heart wasn't ready to let go yet. They walked along, not talking for a minute or two.

"I can't believe you're leaving tomorrow already. It seems like you just got here five minutes ago," Hillary whimpered, finally breaking their silence.

"I know," Rachel replied, mimicking Hillary's tone. "I don't want to leave you. But I don't know how you stand the weather here. You should transfer to a school in Arizona so we can be closer." Hillary smiled at the idea, but she knew she'd never follow through with it. She was a New England girl. She knew she'd never leave.

They carried on talking as they walked quickly to get to the house and out of the cold. Hillary suggested they make use of the living room for the afternoon to talk. Hillary wanted to hear more about whatever happened with the veterinarian Rachel broke up with. They were laughing as they made their way into the house from the back yard.

"What's so funny ladies?" Keith was standing in the kitchen, leaning against the corner of the center island. Hillary stopped laughing immediately on hearing his voice. His position put him in the way of both the back stairs and the hallway to the front stairs. Rachel's laughter died off more slowly, but her face dropped as soon as she saw Hillary go rigid.

"Nothing," Rachel shot back harshly. She pivoted to walk past Keith. As Hillary expected, he shifted his girth into her path. She came to an abrupt stop. Hillary felt herself cowering behind her friend. Rachel lifted her chin defiantly. "Excuse me," she said curtly, again trying to move past him. Keith edged again into her path.

"Where you running off to in such a hurry?" he asked. "Not very friendly of you."

"I wasn't trying to be friendly," Rachel responded sharply. "I know what you did to my friend. Now if you'll get out of our way."

"Wow, this one's got some sass," Keith said, looking at Hillary. "I like a little spunk." This remark he directed back at Rachel. Rachel's face contorted in disgust.

"Right, like that would ever happen," Rachel retorted sarcastically with a sharp laugh. Her stance was firm and she kept her chin raised.

"I could make it happen," Keith said suggestively, moving still closer to Rachel. Her petite frame was at best half the size of his. Hillary could see the fierceness in her friend's eyes as she faced off with Keith. Hillary wished she had half of Rachel's grit.

"Not on your life," Rachel said. To Hillary's surprise, Rachel took a step closer to Keith. The two were nearly toe to toe at this point.

Before she could think about what she was doing, Hillary walked briskly behind Rachel. She hooked her arm through Rachel's and whisked her off toward the hallway to the front stairs.

"If you'll excuse us, we have to get going," Hillary said sarcastically as she pulled Rachel past Keith and down the hallway.

"If that creep ever comes near you again," Rachel started as they made their way up the stairs to Hillary's room.

"I know, Rachel," Hillary replied.

Hillary unlocked the door to her room and they rushed inside, both shaking from the encounter.

"I can't believe you live here with that creep in the house," Rachel said.

"Most of the time, he's in the basement. I never see him," Hillary explained.

"Except the time he almost assaulted you," Rachel pointed out.

"The term is done in just a few weeks. Then there should be other places available and I can look for something else. But for right now, this is what I have." Hillary raised her arms, gesturing to the room.

Rachel let out a heavy sigh. "Fine. But I'm buying you mace," Rachel insisted. Hillary smiled at her friend's concern.

"Fine. If it'll make you feel better," Hillary conceded. "We'll pick some up on the way to your train tomorrow. But for now, I want to hear more about this veterinarian."

Rachel laughed and rolled her eyes. They spent the rest of the afternoon gossiping in Hillary's room. It was like they were back in college again. In their over cramped dorm room. Hillary missed Rachel already and she hadn't even left yet.

But she was glad she kept the rest of what she knew about Keith to herself.

19

Evelyn set aside the plate from her sandwich. She decided to skip dinner in the dining room this evening. She couldn't wait another minute. Evelyn made a sandwich as soon as she arrived home, despite Beatrice's protests and offers to make her up a plate of the chicken she'd roasted for dinner. The food smelled delicious, but Evelyn couldn't possibly wait. She picked one of the diaries out of the bag at random. Normally Evelyn would be more methodical, try to identify a chronological order to the six small books in the canvas tote from the woman with the historical society. But Evelyn was too eager to dig in.

The first book had a floral design printed on the cover with a small monogram. Evelyn could feel her hands shaking, in anticipation, as she opened the cover, gently. She turned past the first few pages before reaching the first entry. The handwriting was a beautiful, sweeping script. Evelyn took in the penmanship. No one writes like that anymore. The first entry was dated 1941. The author wrote with longing for a sweetheart who had been called away to the war. Evelyn found herself feeling a little awkward as she read. The writing was so deeply intimate, Evelyn felt she was intruding. This wasn't the portion of Miss Brown's history she'd been looking for. So Evelyn only lightly skimmed the pages. She would let Miss Brown keep her secrets. Evelyn turned a few pages, reading just a few lines here and there as she paged through the entries. The last entry in this little journal caught her attention. The paper was wrinkled, and the handwriting blotted here and there. Evelyn realized the marks were tear stains. Evelyn glanced at the date and started to read. The sweetheart Miss Brown spoke of with intense, yet innocent affection had been killed in action and wasn't coming home. Her hopes of marriage to this young man had been shattered. Evelyn took in the heartache Miss Brown poured out over the final pages. Her own heart broke a little for this devastated young woman.

Evelyn laid the journal aside. She looked at the remaining five diaries in the tote bag. Evelyn wondered if she should go on reading. Could she go on reading? She wanted to uncover what happened to the former owners of her current residence. But there was something intrusive about reading these diaries. These were Miss Brown's most intimate thoughts. Secrets she kept. Things she probably didn't share with anyone else. Evelyn decided to take a short break before she went on. She took her plate back to the kitchen.

When she returned, Evelyn settled herself back into her oversized chair. She took the remaining five diaries from the bag and set them carefully on her side table. She selected the next volume at random. This volume was from earlier days, the late 30s. Evelyn paged through it quickly. The beautiful handwriting detailed a young girl's gossip from the school room. Evelyn smiled here and there at Miss Brown's musings.

She picked up the next volume. This one contained the fears and doubts of Miss Brown as a first-time mother. Evelyn noticed there was very little mention of her husband among her entries. They mainly focused on the arrival of the baby and detailed his every coo and gurgle. Evelyn felt a light pang of regret as she read Miss Brown's words. They were so full of hope. Evelyn placed this book aside after reading only a few entries.

Evelyn glanced as the clock. It was getting late. The house was quiet. She thought about turning in for the night. She could finish the others the following day. But something urged Evelyn to go on. She decided on a cup of coffee to keep herself going and went down to the kitchen. Beatrice retired for the evening. The kitchen was cleaned and only the light above the stove was left on. By the sound of it, Dr. Immerman must have retired early. There was no glow coming down the hall from the living room, where he often read in the evenings. She didn't hear any conversation. Hillary and her friend must be out somewhere. Evelyn poured her coffee and went back up the back stairs, to her room. She settled back into her chair, pulling her fleece throw over her lap.

Evelyn studied the now smaller pile of diaries left on her table. One of them had to hold the key to what happened to the Brown family. Evelyn felt herself drawn to one of the remaining diaries more so than the others. There was a sheen to the cover the others didn't have. Evelyn drew it out of the pile. She sipped her coffee and let out a sigh as she opened the cover. Across the title page was written in the same even, neat penmanship, the year. 1950.

Evelyn quickly set down her coffee. Here is was! Evelyn's breath caught in excitement. She settled in and turned the page. She started eagerly reading the first entry, her concern for Miss Brown's privacy suddenly gone. The naïve, sweet tone of the previous diaries was not present. This entry was from a careworn woman, disenchanted with her marriage. The entry complained of a disinterested husband who didn't pay her any attention. His focus was entirely on a business venture that wasn't named in the entry.

Evelyn read on. The following entries were more of the same. The charities she served no longer held interest for her. Her friends were becoming consumed with their own marriages and motherhood. Miss Brown was feeling bored, trapped, and frustrated with her lot in life. Then things turned darker. She complained to her husband about needing a change of pace. Maybe they could take a house on the shore that summer. He'd become angry, raised his voice to her. He'd told her she didn't deserve a house on the shore. A few entries later, he was upset at their son's toys being left around the house. Then her own insecurities about her appearance because her husband accused her of not keeping up her figure.

Evelyn was completely engrossed. She devoured each page as the accounts of verbal abuse and insults turned to physical abuse. He'd slapped her when she'd made a retort when he'd complained about her not ironing his shirts properly. Evelyn felt an overwhelming sense of empathy as she read entries where Miss Brown detailed evidence she'd found of her husband's infidelity. He wasn't even attempting to hide his indiscretions.

Miss Brown apparently decided to turn to her mother. An entry detailed a trip Miss Brown took to her parents' home. Evelyn paused, realizing this entry was likely written in a room in the house where she now sat. She wondered which bedroom belonged to Miss Brown. It was quite possibly written in the very room where she now sat. It was only one line in the entry, but it jumped out at Evelyn as she read. Her parents took in a boarder. He arrived a few days before Miss Brown. Evelyn found herself taking a deep breath as she turned the page.

Miss Brown spent a few days with her parents, according to the diary entries. But the tone of her writing suddenly changed completely. The battered and beleaguered housewife was suddenly cheerful and optimistic, full of promise. In the span of just a few days, she had fallen in love with a Captain in the army, boarding with her parents.

20

Hillary had a morning appointment with her advisor. Thanks to her underwhelming writing, her advisor refused to move the meeting. Rachel decided to sleep in. She booked a late flight back so they could have the day together before she had to leave. Hillary's meeting with her advisor consisted of another lecture about her poetry being too mushy and a scolding that she needed to be more disciplined in her writing if she was going to remain in good standing. Hillary went to the library, to work on her portfolio for a while. Rachel would meet her there so they could head to the coffee shop.

Rachel was running late as she made her way to the library. She wasn't even sure where to find Hillary once she got there and Hillary wasn't answering her texts. Rachel couldn't help feeling a little guilty for backing out on their plans to go to grad school together. But she couldn't spend another two to three years of her life feeling trapped. Her mother had been pushing for her to get her doctorate. Her sister finished law school last year at the top of her class. She'd had her pick of the top firms. Their mother was so proud. But Rachel wanted to find her own way. She'd spent her entire life trying to live up to someone else's expectations. She realized she didn't know herself or what she really wanted at all. So, when she saw the posting to work at the farm, she applied before she had time to think. She had to get away; no regrets.

Rachel found the library building and walked inside. She checked her phone again. Still no reply from Hillary. Rachel strolled casually, looking for tables or somewhere Hillary might be working. She didn't see her anywhere. Rachel just started down another aisle when she spotted Hillary's neighbor, Evelyn, with a cart of books to be placed back on shelves.

"Good morning, Evelyn," Rachel greeted her, remembering to keep her voice low. "I'm supposed to meet Hillary here. Have you seen her?"

"I haven't seen her. But if she's here, she usually finds a corner up on third floor," Evelyn said, not bothering to speak in a lower tone.

"Thanks," Rachel replied, matching her tone. She hesitated a minute. "Evelyn, can I ask you something?" Evelyn went back to putting books away.

"Sure," Evelyn replied, not looking away from her task.

"Hillary and I ran into the landlord in your building the other morning and he really gave me the creeps," she explained.

"Is there a question in there?" Evelyn asked, still not looking away from the books she was putting away.

"I'm just wondering if Hillary is safe living there. She had a run in with him a while back," Rachel replied.

"We don't generally see much of Keith," Evelyn started. "He generally stays in his apartment in the basement. His aunt handles the day to day around the house."

"His aunt?" Rachel asked.

"Beatrice, the housekeeper," Evelyn replied like it should be perfectly obvious. "She's Keith's aunt. She cooks and cleans. Very sweet woman. She feels it's her responsibility to look out for Keith."

"Has Keith ever hurt anyone?" Rachel asked before she could stop herself. She really didn't want to hear the answer.

"He spent some time in prison but that was a long time ago. I don't remember what he did. I know Beatrice told me once, but I don't remember," Evelyn. "I don't think it was for anything violent. Embezzlement maybe." Rachel stopped listening after Evelyn said the word prison. Her best friend was living in a house with convict. What could Hillary possibly be thinking?

"Okay, well I better go find Hillary," Rachel replied awkwardly, shifting her weight. "Thanks." She turned quickly and found her way to the stairs. Her adrenaline was pumping and she needed to burn off the excess energy. She made her way up the stairs to the third floor. Hillary sat at a table in the corner, flooded in morning light from the windows. It was quiet and no one else was around.

"There you are," Hillary said brightly as she spotted her friend.

"Sorry," Rachel replied. "I was running late and then I wasn't sure where you would be. I tried to text you."

"Oh, sorry," Hillary answered, reaching into her bag on the floor for her phone. "I silenced my phone for my meeting and forgot to pull it back out." She checked the screen, finding Rachel's texts.

"How was your meeting?" Rachel asked.

"She basically said if I don't get it together, I'm going to be kicked out of school," Hillary said glumly.

"Oh come on," Rachel replied. "I'm sure she didn't say that."

"Not in so many words," Hillary admitted, "but she thinks my poetry is garbage. And I'm weeks behind on my other writing."

"I've read your poetry before," Rachel replied. "It can't be that bad." Hillary pulled a folio out of her bag and handed it across the table to her.

"Here," she said. "See for yourself."

Rachel rolled her eyes as she took the folio from Hillary. She turned a few pages to one of the poems. The smirk on her face at her friend's unjustified self-doubt suddenly fell as she read the piece. This was not the work of the friend she knew. Hillary was a talented writer. This sounded like it was written by a twelve-year-old with her first crush. Rachel glanced up at her friend and then back down at the page. She couldn't bring herself to finish it. Rachel turned to the next piece. It was even worse. She closed the folio, studying the front cover as she tried to gather her thoughts.

"This is," Rachel stopped. She didn't know what to say. The work was awful. "Maybe it just needs," she couldn't find the words. "What is going on with you?" she finally asked.

"It's horrible, isn't it?" Hillary looked crushed.

"Hil, this isn't you," Rachel started. "You don't write hearts and flowers, moon and June, mush." Rachel gave up on being diplomatic. "Is this because of that guy in your building? He is really messing with your head."

"Yeah, I guess so," Hillary sighed. "Hillary glanced at the time. "We should get going. I need some coffee." Rachel smiled sympathetically at her friend.

"It's going to be okay. You'll figure it out," Rachel said, trying to be reassuring as Hillary packed up her bag.

"I better," Hillary smirked.

"You will," Rachel replied, putting her arm around her, with a reassuring squeeze, as they made their way to the stairs.

21

Hillary was coming back up the stairs after taking the first of Rachel's bags down to her car. Rachel was finishing packing up the second bag. She had never been one to pack light. Hillary was fighting the feeling of melancholy as she made her way back to her room. Rachel would need help with the rest of her luggage. She really didn't want Rachel to leave. Hillary pulled her arms tighter around herself as she started down the hallway to her room. She shivered slightly.

"You're in a hurry," Robert said, making Hillary jump. She hadn't seen him standing there.

"I'm sorry," Hillary said, trying to sound cheerful. "I guess my mind was elsewhere." She kept her arms wrapped tightly around herself. There was a chill in the hallway.

"You look unhappy," he observed. "Is something wrong?"

"My best friend has been in town for a visit but she's going home today," Hillary replied. She was surprised he noticed her mood.

"I had a best friend once," he replied, sounding a little sad. Hillary was a little confused by this remark. When she'd run into Robert before he always seemed so confident and self-assured. The idea that Robert didn't have friends was strange to her.

"My friend Rachel is just in my room," Hillary said. "Would you like to meet her?"

"Hey Hil, can you give me a hand with this," Rachel called from down the hall. Hillary's head turned sharply toward Rachel. She was trying to wrestle her bags out of Hillary's door.

"Sure, in a second," Hillary called back. "First come meet my neighbor." Hillary turned back to Robert. He looked uncomfortable, shifting nervously.

"Okay, in a second. First let me just get this thing into the hall," Rachel called back. Hillary turned back toward Rachel and started toward her to urge her over to meet Robert. She took a few steps before she stopped herself and turned back to Robert. But Robert wasn't there. Hillary glanced toward the door to his room, staring at it a long moment. She hadn't heard the latch.

"Where's your neighbor?" Rachel asked, finally standing behind Hillary.

"He was just here," Hillary said, slightly dumbfounded, still staring at the door.

"Are you sure?" Rachel asked.

"Of course I'm sure," Hillary snapped. "I was just talking to him."

"Okay, okay, I'm sorry," Rachel said. "I was trying to get my bags out into the hall."

"It's fine," Hillary responded, finally looking at her friend. The disappointment was plain across her face.

"It's clearly not fine," Rachel said. "You're standing here, pissed at me because I didn't come rushing right over to meet your neighbor."

"That's not why I'm upset," Hillary retorted. "All I asked was for him to meet my friend and he freaked out and went back in his room."

"Hillary, listen to yourself. You're talking about him like he has some kind of boyfriend obligation to meet your friends. You're not dating this guy."

"I know," Hillary responded, defeated. "I know I'm not dating him."

"I'm getting worried," Rachel went on. "You're obsessed with this guy who doesn't give you the time of day. You're basically failing out of school. And your neighbor told me your landlord apparently did time." Hillary looked at Rachel, not saying anything. "You knew about that, didn't you?"

"Yes," Hillary admitted. "Beatrice told me."

"Anything else you're not telling me about your creepy landlord who tried to assault you in the kitchen?" Rachel demanded. Hillary looked away, sucking in her lips.

"When I went down to his apartment in the basement, to pay my rent, I heard him yelling at his wife. From what I heard, I think he hit her," Hillary said avoiding eye contact. "They have a little boy. Tommy. He's six."

"Are you kidding me?!" Rachel responded incredulously. "Hillary. What are you doing living here?!"

"There are other people here. It's not like I'm alone," Hillary responded, annoyed. "And I told you. There aren't any other housing options right now."

"Whatever," Rachel said throwing up her hands. "I'm not going to argue with you, but you have to move out of this place." Rachel turned back toward Hillary's room to get her bags. Hillary remained where she was a minute longer, looking back at Robert's door. Then she went down the hall to help Rachel. As they wrestled her bags down the hall, Rachel gestured toward Robert's door. "You better not be staying here because of that guy."

"I'm not," Hillary snapped, struggling with the bag she was carrying.

They didn't talk as they made their way down the back stairs and out to Hillary's car. They loaded Rachel's bags and drove in silence toward the train station. What started out as a perfect weekend was falling apart. Hillary fumed as she drove. She was not staying in the house because of Robert. Sure, he was handsome, and she was really hoping something was going to change. But she wasn't staying there for him. Keith was a scummy creep, but she couldn't just leave the house knowing what she knew. She had to find some way to help Dottie. There had to be something she could do. She didn't believe she, herself, was in any actual danger. And so what if her writing had been a little off lately? All writers went through periods like that. What business was it of Rachel's? Afterall, she's the one who ran away. Hillary was so lost in her own thoughts; she missed her exit.

"I think you were supposed to turn back there," Rachel finally said. Hillary glanced at her, annoyed.

"I know. I'll turn around," Hillary replied flatly.

"I'm really sorry if I made you angry," Rachel finally said. "I know I didn't hold up my end of the deal. But I needed to get out here. I was suffocating here. I finally feel like myself in Arizona. I'm happy there. And you need to focus on what makes you happy. You love writing."

Hillary stared out the windshield as she drove on to the next exit to turn around. She didn't know what to say. She was angry with Rachel, but she also knew she was right.

"I'll get it figured out," she responded as she merged back onto the interstate, toward the exit she missed. "This has just been really hard."

"I know," Rachel replied quietly. "Maybe you can come spend winter break with me. Maybe I can find you a nice veterinarian."

Hillary smiled lightly at Rachel's joke. "I'd like that."

22

The library was quiet now that winter break started. Evelyn had plenty to catch up on before the Spring term started. But it could wait an hour or two. She felt so close to piecing together the rest of this puzzle. The last of Miss Brown's diaries hadn't contained much of use to her. Evelyn's speculation was in overdrive. Did she run off with the charming Captain? It would be a romantic ending to this little mystery, but it still didn't explain why the house was abandoned. Maybe there was something more sinister to all this. The question was, what?

Evelyn was back in the research room. Her interns all left for the winter break. She savored the peace and quiet as she sipped an afternoon coffee. She was all alone with her research. Just the way she liked it. Evelyn decided to turn to the police blotters next. The Browns' daughter made reference to her husband's abuse. Domestic disturbances weren't something people called the police about in those days but maybe there was something. It was probably a long shot, but she virtually exhausted all her other options. The diaries were a lucky find but they still didn't answer her question.

This was one area that was time consuming to search. The filters were limited and if she restricted it too far, the database would give no results at all. Evelyn tended to avoid looking for information this way. It tended to be a waste of time. But she was running out of ideas. She skimmed through a seemingly endless list of police calls. It hardly seemed possible there could be so many. Evelyn hesitated to skip past pages in the records, for fear she'd overlook the one thing she was looking for. She was just about to get up to make another cup of coffee when she finally found it. A call to the Maple Street house. Based on the timeline she'd made from the diaries, it was shortly after Miss Brown visited and found herself smitten with the Captain. It was a domestic disturbance. Evelyn sat back and studied the details. It would be highly unusual for someone to make a domestic disturbance call at the time. The blotter didn't provide many details about the circumstances. But this was the Browns. Evelyn jotted down the date and time of the call. She pulled up another database and went to refill her coffee.

When she returned to her place, she ran another search. A police call to the Brown home would certainly have made headlines. Or had it? Would the Browns have been influential enough to keep their dirty laundry out of the papers? Evelyn started running through search terms. Her first few attempts yielded nothing. But then she found it. An article published in what must have been the only paper in town not in William Junior's pocket.

The article detailed police being called to the Brown home over a disagreement between the Browns' son-in-law and an unnamed person residing in the house. A photo showed an old squad car parked in front of the picket fence of the Maple Street house. The details of the incident were very limited. There had been a physical altercation between the two young men. But the reason wasn't stated. Neighbors interviewed reported shouting and a physical altercation in the gardens of the house. It was one of the neighbors who called the police. None of the neighbors were quoted about anything that was said during the fight.

Evelyn sat back, imagining fisticuffs between the rumbled mess of a groom from the Browns' daughter's wedding photo and the clean-cut, classic, all-American, Captain. She imagined Mrs. Brown watching from a window in the dining room, wringing her hands. Maybe William Junior trying to break it up, out in the yard. It would have been quite the scene. Evelyn had a hard time imagining the son-in-law getting jealous enough to confront the Captain. But that wasn't really the point, was it? He wasn't jealous. Not in that way, anyway. Evelyn imagined he considered his wife property, a status symbol. She elevated his social standing, but he didn't love her. If he lost her, he lost his position. That was what he cared about. Or at least that was what Evelyn imagined he cared about.

If the Brown's daughter's husband turned up at his in-law's home to confront the Captain, he must have found out about his wife's feelings for the Captain. Did he read her diaries? Had she taken all she was going to of his abuse and threatened to leave? Evelyn wondered what it had taken to send him into such a rage. And if he came to settle a score with the Captain, what had he done to her before he left for his in-law's house? Evelyn suddenly felt a cold shiver run through her body. She looked for the obituaries for William Senior and William Junior, but she hadn't thought to look for one for Miss Brown. Was she still alive when this happened? Evelyn shivered again. Nothing in the article indicated there was any further investigation into the incident. She made a few notes and closed down the article.

Evelyn went back to the blotter records and continued to skim. She didn't have an address for the Browns' daughter after her marriage, but she obviously hadn't remained living in her family home. Evelyn looked more carefully at the names in the records, looking for anything involving Miss Brown. Nothing caught Evelyn's attention.

Evelyn started drumming her fingers on the keyboard in frustration. There was something here. She was so close to figuring it out. Evelyn picked up her cup as she advanced to the next page of records. She kept skimming as she sipped. It seemed ridiculous to keep looking. But she wasn't ready to give up just yet. She moved on to the next page. Something about three lines down caught Evelyn's attention. She pulled up the record to get a better look. What she read next nearly made her drop her cup.

23

Hillary used her job at the coffee shop as an excuse to avoid traveling to Florida to see her parents for Hanukkah. She actually wasn't working many hours. The coffee shop wasn't busy when classes weren't in session. Hillary decided she better use the time to clean up her portfolio. Her advisor warned her she could be dropped from the program if she didn't do something about her work. It was the wakeup call she needed. She had been spending most of her days locked away in her room, writing. Hillary was tucked under a blanket in front of her computer, watching fluffy snowflakes gently falling outside her window. It was the inspiration she'd needed, and she felt better about her portfolio.

Hillary's coffee had gone cold but she didn't want to get out from under her blanket to get another cup. She was trying to convince herself to go down to the kitchen when it occurred to her that her rent was due. Her stomach twisted with the feeling of dread. Dr. Immerman was away for the holiday. Evelyn would be at the library. Hillary assumed she would be working fewer hours too, with no students around. But she was obsessing about the research project she was working on. According to Evelyn, a wealthy family owned the house a long time ago, but they abandoned it. She thought it had something to do with an army Captain who boarded with the family when he came back from Korea. Hillary thought Robert was in the military, judging by the uniform he always seemed to be wearing when she saw him. How ironic would it be if the room he lived in now was the same room this Captain lived in back then? Evelyn had been really excited about getting her hands on some diaries that belonged to the daughter of the family. But apparently, they had been another dead end to figuring out what happened to the family. Hillary thought the whole thing sounded like it would make a great novel or a sappy movie, maybe. She was enjoying the distraction.

Speaking of Robert, she hadn't seen him since Rachel's visit. His disappearing act finally put her off him completely, at least for the time being. But at the moment, she would feel better about having to go pay her rent if she knew someone else was in the house. She glanced at the time again. Beatrice would likely be somewhere around, cleaning or more likely shredding potatoes for latkas, for dinner.

Hillary gathered up her rent, her coffee cup, and the plate from her lunch. This would be a quick errand and she could come right back to the safety of her room. Still she could feel her adrenaline starting to pulse. Beatrice was at the counter as Hillary made her way down the stairs, into the kitchen. She was hand shredding potatoes. Hillary smiled. Something about Beatrice always reminded her of her *bubbe*. Especially now. She always insisted on hand shredding her potatoes too. Wouldn't hear of using a food processor. Hillary warmed at the memory.

"There you are, dear," Beatrice greeted her. "You've been so quiet, I almost forgot anyone else was here."

"I have a lot of work to do before Spring term starts," Hillary explained.

"I'll fry the fish just before dinner tonight. The *sufganiyot* are rising. I'll fry them up next. Always so much extra to do for a holiday," Beatrice went on, continuing her work on the potatoes. Pieces stuck to her fingers as she continued shredding.

"It's really nice of you to do all this," Hillary replied.

"Oh, I don't mind, dear," Beatrice smiled. "I enjoy these recipes. And this time of year feels less lonely with all of you to cook for."

"You're welcome to join us for candle lighting this evening, if you'd like," Hillary said.

"Oh that's alright, dear," Beatrice responded.

"I have to go downstairs to pay my rent. Is Keith in?" Hillary asked.

"I think I heard him," she responded, wiping pieces of shredded potato from her fingers on a flour sack towel.

"Thanks," Hillary responded, leaving her plate in the sink and setting her coffee cup next to the pot. She'd refill it before she went back upstairs. Beatrice would likely already have it prepared for her when she came back up. Hillary paused at the top of the basement stairs. She took a deep breath, wondering if she would ever not get the creeps from having to walk down these stairs. She listened a second. All was quiet. She started down slowly.

"Is anything ever good enough for you?" shouted a male voice as Hillary reached the fourth or fifth step. She stopped. "You wouldn't be happy if we lived in a damn palace, would you? You'd want a bigger one."

"That's not what I meant," a woman responded with a shaky voice.

"Oh, that's not what you meant" he mocked. "It's never what you meant. Must be so nice to never say what you mean."

"I'm sorry," the woman said quietly.

"Just like you always are. You're always sorry about something. When you're not harping on me about dumb shit like this," his anger was rising. Hillary didn't move.

"Please don't," the woman responded.

"Please don't, please don't, please don't," the male mocked again. "It's always please don't. How about you don't tell me what the hell to do." Hillary heard the woman crying but no response. "Work my ass off and all I do is get harped on and nagged. How about you just shut the hell up? And there you go with that goddamn crying again. Just a like a baby! All you do is nag and whine and cry. I'm fucking sick of listening to it. Don't know why I even stay here. I should just leave your ass. Then let's see how you survive. You couldn't make it. Wouldn't last a week and you'd be begging me to come back. Maybe I'll do that. Maybe I'll just walk out that door."

"Please stop," the woman pleaded.

"Or maybe I should just kick you out. Throw your whining ass out on the street. I'll leave the shed unlocked. You can go live in there. Shouldn't be that bad this time of year. Then let's see how bad living here really is." His voice suddenly came down from shouting to a serious speaking tone. "That's what I'll do. I'll let you live out in the shed for a week. Then maybe you'll learn to appreciate everything I do for you. Maybe then you'll manage to keep this place clean. I think I like this plan. I really do." Hillary could hear the woman sobbing.

"Please don't make me live in the shed. I can do better," the woman pleaded meekly.

"Oh, you don't want to live in the shed? Why don't you beg me to let you keep living in the house? Go on, beg me. I want to hear you beg. And maybe I'll let you stay in the house. So you don't freeze to death out in the shed. Not that you deserve to live in the house," he replied. He paused his rant. "Come on. I don't hear any begging. Get on your goddamn knees and let me hear you beg me." Hillary heard something fall against the floor like he shoved her down.

"Please, please let me stay in the house. I don't want to live in the shed," she sobbed.

"Hmm, not good enough," he responded. "You have to make me believe it, you dumb bitch." Hillary heard the sound of a slap. She shuddered as if the blow had been delivered to her own face. How did Beatrice hear this day in and day out and do nothing about it?

"Please don't send me out to live in the shed," the woman was sobbing harder now, choking out her words.

"Better but not quite good enough. What would make it better? Oh, I know. Call me your lord and master," his voice growling. "That'll make it better. After all, I own your ass. You'd be nothing without me keeping a roof over your head. I want to hear you beg your lord and master to let you stay in this house." The woman was weeping pitifully.

"Please, my lord and master," came the choking sobs. "Please let me stay." Hillary could taste the bitter bile rising in the back of her throat. She couldn't keep listening to this. She had to make him stop.

"Well, lucky for you your lord and master is feeling generous today. Now quit your fucking crying and make me my goddamn meal." Hillary heard another slap. The woman sobbed in relief. Then Hillary heard the shuffling sounds of someone getting up from the floor. She waited. Just as Hillary finally reached Keith's door, she heard his lumbering, heavy footsteps. "You started on that damn dinner yet? Or are you still whining and moaning on the floor?" Hillary heard him shout. Hillary couldn't stand by and let him start up again. She knocked on the door, hard.

She heard the lumbering, shuffling steps again but they sounded farther from the door than they should have been. She waited. The bolt slid from its lock and the door opened.

"What," Keith demanded, leaning heavily on the door frame. Hillary marveled at how he always looked like he'd been half asleep after what she just heard. There was no sound or movement in the apartment behind him.

"Is everything okay?" she stammered. Her heart was racing.

"Why don't you mind your own damn business?" Keith responded calmly. She glared at him. "Was there something else you wanted? Or did you just come down here to butt in?"

"I brought my rent," she responded holding out the envelope, maintaining her glare.

Keith snatched the envelope and closed the door without another word. Hillary remained motionless as she listened to the bolt snap back into place. She listened to Keith shuffle back across the floor. Then nothing. Finally she turned and went back up the stairs.

24

Hillary was shaking as she made her way back up to her room. She was so distracted from what she heard in the basement, she breezed right past Beatrice without a word. How could she stand by and allow her nephew to treat his wife that way? And that poor little boy, living in that environment. Hillary wondered if Keith ever raised a hand to his son. Had little Tommy learned to hide when his father behaved that way? What did Dottie tell him about his father's tempers? Hillary's mind was racing as she rushed to her room. What could she do? She had to do something. Could she call the police? Would child services do anything to help? It would be her word against his. No one else was willing to say anything if they hadn't by now. And Hillary didn't have any proof. If Dottie wasn't willing to make a statement or press charges against him, was there even anything Hillary could do?

She paced around her room. Hillary knew Rachel would be upset with her if she put herself in harm's way. She couldn't put herself at risk. And after what happened with Keith, in the kitchen, she was too afraid to confront him herself. But she couldn't sit idly by while that monster treated his wife like that. There must be something she could do. Hillary realized she forgot her coffee. It was the perfect excuse to go back down to the kitchen. She could at least say something to Beatrice. She was his aunt. There must be something she could do to help. After all, she'd said her nephew needed to exercise his demons, whatever that meant. Maybe she could be persuaded to do something. If Keith had been in prison, shouldn't he have a parole officer or someone Beatrice could contact? Hillary took a deep breath and went back down to the kitchen.

"There you are, dear," Beatrice said. "I made you a fresh cup, but you sailed through here so quickly, I didn't have a chance to point it out."

"I'm sorry," Hillary said quickly, retrieving the cup from the counter. "Beatrice, I heard something in the basement, just now, when I went to make my rent payment."

"What's that dear?" Beatrice asked. She was filling *sufganiyot* with jelly. Her fingers covered in the sugar coating.

"It sounded like an argument," Hillary responded. She was fighting the urge to be accusatory or confrontational.

"Oh that," Beatrice responded, setting down the piping bag and wiping her hands. She looked Hillary squarely in the eye. "Don't trouble yourself about that, dear." Her tone remained friendly and sweet.

"I'm sorry. What?" Hillary asked, shocked.

"It's just Keith's way," she responded casually.

"It's just Keith's way?! Beatrice, what are you talking about?" Hillary started. She was about to go on when Beatrice abruptly put a hand up to stop her.

"I said, don't trouble yourself about it," Beatrice cut her off in a more direct tone this time. Hillary opened her mouth to reply but Beatrice's stare made her close her mouth before she could make any sound. Hillary turned and made her way back up the stairs.

Hillary was in a state of shock as she reached the hallway to her room. She couldn't believe Beatrice's indifference. She knew what was going on in the basement and she'd told Hillary not to trouble herself with it. She shivered at the thought of what was happening to Dottie. Hillary realized she was staring into her coffee cup on her way down the hall. She glanced up and there was Robert.

"Good evening," he greeted her. Normally she would have made polite conversation, but her mood wouldn't allow it. His casual tone, like he hadn't vanished when she tried to introduce him to her friend, set her teeth on edge.

"What's so great about it?" Hillary snapped. Robert looked taken aback at her response.

"I'm sorry?" Robert asked, confused. "Did I say something wrong?"

"Are you serious right now?" Hillary demanded.

"I am, I'm afraid. I'm not sure what I did," Robert replied.

"Every time I talk to you, you disappear. I wanted to introduce you to my friend, you vanish. Evelyn comes up the stairs, you're gone. What exactly is your deal?"

"I'm sorry. I don't understand," Robert replied.

Hillary responded before she had time to think. "I like you," she blurted out. "Okay. I know we've only talked a few times and every time anyone else comes around, you seem to disappear. Maybe you're just really shy or something. But I'm the type of person who doesn't speak up about things and today I just can't do that. So I like you and I would like to go out with you. There it is and now it's out there. Robert, I like you."

They stood in the hallway, looking at each other. Not talking. Her words were out there and she couldn't take them back. Hillary started to panic, realizing what she had just done. She had never done anything like that before. She also realized he wasn't saying anything. He just stood there, looking at her. She tried to read his expression. All she could discern was a blank stare. She couldn't read his face. This was a disaster. He was supposed to say something. Say he liked her too. Apologize that he'd been shy or hadn't spoken up to her. Whatever made things complicated before was over and why didn't they go out for a walk in the snowy night. And it would start snowing again, softly. The big, fat flakes that looked so magical as they danced gently to the ground. Instead this man she just bore her soul to was just standing there. And he wasn't saying anything.

"Hillary, I am very sorry if I have given you the wrong impression," he replied, finally breaking the silence. "My heart belongs to someone else and I have to be loyal to her."

Hillary was crushed. She took a chance. For once in her life, she put herself out there. And he turned her down. All the events of the afternoon converged at once, causing Hillary's eyes to brim with tears. Her eyes spilled over as she rushed past Robert, down the hall, to her room. Hillary quickly closed the door behind herself, bolting the lock. Then she stood, with her back against the door, as her tears continued to fall.

25

Hilary threw herself into working on her portfolio for the rest of winter break. By the time Spring semester started, her advisor told her she was back on track and off probation. Her weekly conversations with Rachel were getting shorter. She had less to talk about when all she did was schoolwork. Rachel regaled her with tales of her latest conquest. She spent a long weekend with the latest one in Aspen and was considering moving there, to work at a ski resort for a while. When they ended the video chat, Hillary couldn't help but roll her eyes at Rachel's impulsiveness.

Hillary only half listened to Evelyn during dinner. She mused that she was becoming more and more like Dr. Immerman, the longer she lived in the house. Evelyn was working on the final bits of her search and compiling her notes. She seemed really excited about her project, but Hillary could hardly bring herself to listen. She hadn't seen Robert since their last run in. She used the front stairs as often as could, to avoid possibly running into him again. Beatrice seemed to avoid her after Hillary tried to talk to her about Keith and Dottie.

With school back in session, Hillary was getting more hours at the coffee shop. The work helped fill the hours when she wasn't in seminars or working on her portfolio. She really didn't do much of anything else. Rachel was getting on her case about needing to socialize more but Hillary just didn't want to. She was working a morning shift before her afternoon seminar when Dr. Immerman came in with his newspaper. He usually stopped by once a week for a coffee before his mid-day office hours.

"You seem to be keeping yourself busy lately," Dr. Immerman observed after ordering his usual.

"I had some issues staying on track last semester," she explained as she started on his drink. "It took me all of winter break, but I'm finally back on track."

"That's good to hear. I would hate to think that run in with our landlord derailed your work," he responded. They hadn't spoken of the incident since Dr. Immerman left her room that morning. Hillary preferred not to think about it. She smiled lightly, avoiding eye contact. "You seem to be spending a lot of time working lately. What are you writing? I'd ask at dinner, but Ms. Berke won't stop going on about that project she's working on about the history of the house."

"I had to scrap all of the poetry I wrote last term. My advisor said it was overly juvenile," she responded. If Hillary wasn't mistaken, she thought she saw Dr. Immerman crack a hint of a smile at her remark. "Now that I'm finished with that, I've been working on some short stories. I'm hoping one of them will spark an idea for a novel."

"I have a book I should loan you. If you're aspiring to be a historical fiction writer, you may find it helpful," he replied. Hillary looked at him a long moment. Was he actually offering to help her?

"Thank you," she answered. "I appreciate that."

"A colleague of mine wrote it. The story might appeal to you if have an interest in writing historical fiction centered around a major war. This one is set around World War I." He wasn't much of a salesman, but Hillary didn't want to be rude.

"That sounds interesting," she responded, handing him his coffee. He raised it in a gesture of gratitude.

"I'll have to find it for you. I'll bring it down to dinner this evening." Hillary smiled in thanks as he turned and made his way to a table.

She busied herself cleaning up before the next customer came in. Once things settled down a bit, Hillary grabbed a bottle of spray cleaner and rag. She started working on cleaning up tables from the morning rush. Dr. Immerman sat at his usual table, near the window, engrossed in the day's headlines. She was deliberate in working on tables at the opposite end of the small dining room area, hoping to avoid further conversation with him. Eventually the tables next to his were the only ones left and she had to move closer.

"Can I get you another coffee, Dr. Immerman?" she asked, hoping he would have a second cup today. Even though he never did. But she was willing to ask in the hopes it would give her an excuse to go back behind the counter and further avoid conversation with him.

"Thank you, no," he replied, looking up from his paper. She smiled politely as she gathered up cups and rubbish left on the table next to his. She had one table left. Hillary thought she managed to dodge further conversation with him, as she gave her last table a final wipe when Dr. Immerman looked up from his paper. "Say, I was wondering," he said, breaking the silence. There was no one else in the shop. "Whatever happened between you and that young man you were going on about?"

Hillary turned away from him, closing her eyes. The last thing she wanted to discuss was Robert. She was still mortified about confronting him. She quickly became defensive when Rachel asked about him, shortly after it happened. She hadn't meant to but the whole thing was so embarrassing, and she didn't want to discuss it. Hillary had been forced to realize Robert never had any interest in her at all, no matter how intriguing she found him. She also had to come to terms with the fact that she knew nothing about him and built a nonexistent relationship in her mind. Nothing was ever going to happen with him.

"Oh, that," Hillary finally replied, trying to sound casual. "It didn't work out." She spit out the words quickly and then walked away before Dr. Immerman could make any reply.

Dr. Immerman watched her go back behind the counter and busy herself with more clean-up. Then he shrugged and went back to his paper.

26

"This was no accident", she thought, as she frantically scanned the article on her phone. Rachel sent it to her with the comment, 'isn't this your neighbor?!'. "I know it wasn't an accident. He's responsible. That pig killed his wife and that sweet little boy."

Hillary continued to scroll through the newspaper article, laying out the details of a deadly car crash, involving Dottie. Her little boy, Tommy, was also in the car. She'd been driving way too fast, in a rural area. The middle of nowhere. The article said she didn't have her headlights on. Officers, quoted in the article, said they were still investigating why the lights were off when they seemed to be in good working order.

"Of course she didn't have her lights on," Hillary thought. "She was running from him."

Dottie had taken a curve too sharply and struck another vehicle head-on. She and Tommy were apparently killed on impact. A blurry, black and white, image of the accident scene showed the mangled wreckage.

Hillary closed her eyes, offering up a silent prayer for Dottie and her little boy. She felt so guilty. Was there something she should have done? She didn't know Dottie very well and only saw her a few times. But she heard the arguments coming up the basement stairs on her way in and out of the house. And poor little Tommy. What a sweet little boy. How awful it must have been for him, growing up with a father who treated his mother that way. Going to bed every night in that damp, musty basement. That's no way for a child to live.

Something in the article caught Hillary's attention. A detail she overlooked before. There were no skid marks coming from Dottie's car and officers thought her brakes failed.

"He cut her brake lines," Hillary said out loud.

Keith knew she was planning to leave him. Taking Tommy and starting over. He didn't want to lose his child or his control over her. So he cut her brake lines.

"That bastard," Hillary growled.

Before she knew what she was doing, Hillary closed the article on her phone and walked out of the library. She wasn't going to let him get away with this. Her anger seethed and she stormed across the lawn in front of the library. Dr. Immerman was walking toward her. It was early afternoon and he was returning to the campus for his afternoon class. He looked at her quizzically.

"Hillary, what's the matter?" he asked, confused by her anger.

"I need to talk to Keith," she responded, not making eye contact with him.

"Keith?" he asked. "Why do you need to talk to him?"

"Because he killed his wife and son," she answered, maintaining her focus straight ahead. Not altering her path.

Dr. Immerman stood, motionless, looking after Hillary as she continued down the street.

"What are you talking about?!" he called after her. Hillary continued walking. Dr. Immerman had to jog to catch up to her. "Hillary, what do you mean he killed his wife and son?! How do you know this?"

She finally glanced in his direction but continued walking. "My friend sent me the article, about the accident Dottie was in a few days ago. She and Tommy were killed in a car crash. The article said her brakes failed. But they didn't fail. He cut them. He cut her brakes and now she's dead. And he's not going to get away with it."

"What are you talking about, Hillary?" Dr. Immerman asked, struggling to keep up with her as she continued to storm down the street. "Are you sure you're feeling alright? Maybe we should go somewhere and talk about this. Let me see this article. You can't just go confront Keith about this."

"I don't have time for that," she snapped back. "I know what he did and I'm going to get him to admit it." Her gaze shifted back to the street in front of her. She wasn't looking at him.

"Look, Keith is a troubled man and I know you've had your issues with him. But he's not violent. I have serious doubts he would kill anyone. I don't know his wife but maybe she was tired, fell asleep behind the wheel. It could happen. You're clearly upset. Let's go somewhere and talk."

Hillary stopped suddenly and turned to him. Dr. Immerman exhaled in relief, thinking he had finally gotten through to her. Hillary stood facing him, not saying anything, blinking.

"What do you mean, you don't know his wife?" she asked, slowly. "You've rented a room in that house for five years. They live in the basement. But you've never met Dottie or Tommy?!"

"I spend a lot of time doing reading and I don't exactly socialize with my landlord," explained Dr. Immerman. "I guess our paths just haven't crossed." Hillary remained motionless, staring at him.

Time seemed to stand still as they studied each other. Dr. Immerman was concerned Hillary was having some sort of mental break. His colleagues shared stories over the years of graduate students buckling under the pressure. Although he had never seen it happen himself. Hillary was baffled, trying to process what Dr. Immerman said about not knowing Dottie or Tommy. It wasn't that big of a house. How does a person simply not cross paths with someone, living in the same house, for five years? It just wasn't possible.

"Hillary, please," Dr. Immerman said, finally breaking the silence. His voice far more calm than he felt. "The coffee shop is a block from here. Let's go there together. You can show me this article and we can decide what to do about your suspicions together."

Hillary didn't move. Her breathing slowed again. She hadn't realized how her heart was racing. She took in his matter of fact, reasonable tone. She realized she didn't have a plan. She couldn't just burst into Keith's apartment and confront him without a plan. Wasn't that how the girl in the scary movie always ended up needing to be rescued? Confronting the villain and ending up in danger herself.

"Hillary," broached Dr. Immerman.

"Okay," she exhaled.

They fell into step beside each other, this time strolling at a casual pace. Neither of them spoke. Hillary felt dizzy, coming down from the adrenaline rush. Maybe Dr. Immerman was right. Maybe Dottie did fall asleep. It was late. She could have been tired. Hillary combed the details from the article over in her mind. There was another car involved. Did the other car cross the centerline? Maybe it wasn't Dottie's fault at all. But her brakes still could have failed in that case. The other car could have come out of nowhere and she tried to brake but the car wouldn't stop. Because Keith cut her brakes. She could feel her heart starting to thunder again just as Dr. Immerman opened the door of the coffee shop, ushering her inside. Her mind was racing.

They placed an order at the counter and sat down at his usual table, near the window. The place was empty, aside from an undergrad with his earbuds in, staring at his laptop. They sat quietly until their drinks arrived. Hillary's thoughts were still racing as she tried to rationalize what she read. Dr. Immerman ordered her chamomile tea. As she inhaled the steam from her cup, she could feel her thoughts begin to settle.

"Okay," said Dr. Immerman, breaking the silence as he set down his cup of coffee. "Why don't you show me this article your friend sent you?"

Hillary pulled her phone from her bag. The article was still up when she unlocked her screen. She flicked the screen to the beginning of the article.

"Here," she responded, handing Dr. Immerman her phone. "It happened a few days ago. Keith treats her terribly. He's been abusing her. I've heard them when I have gone into the basement to pay my rent."

He studied the screen as Hillary continued talking, scrolling as he read. "The photo quality is horrible," he remarked. "I don't remember the last time I saw a black and white photo in a newspaper." His brow knitted as he read back over the caption on the photo. "Hillary, did you look at this caption?"

She studied him for a moment. "I must not have."

His eyes didn't leave her phone screen as he considered the caption again. "It says this Dorothy's car was a 1949. Are you sure this is the same woman you know?"

Confusion washed over Hillary's face. "Of course it's her. There's a picture of her toward the top of the article. I know it's her."

Dr. Immerman scrolled back up toward the top of the article. Dottie and Tommy were smiling together, standing on the front porch steps in front of the Maple Street house in another grainy, black and white, photo. He looked up at Hillary, back at the phone and then back at her.

"What?" Hillary asked. "Do you recognize her now?"

"The caption on this picture says it was taken in 1950," he said, turning the phone so she could see the caption.

Hillary stared a moment, seeing the caption on the photo. It was no mistake. Hillary snatched her phone back, still looking at the caption.

"I…" she stammered, her eyes not leaving the screen. "I have to go." She rushed to her feet, nearly knocking her chair to the floor. She slung her bag over her shoulder and rushed out the door, leaving her steaming cup of tea on the table.

27

None of this made any sense. Hillary met Dottie. She met Tommy. They had been in the house. They went down the basement stairs. Keith yelled at Dottie. She heard him hit her. He abused her and called her names. Keith killed his wife and his son. But if that were the case, then why was the car a 1949 and how was the picture from 1950? Hillary was heading back toward the house. She would have to find somewhere else to stay for a few days while she decided what to do but she was not staying in the house and paying rent to a murderer. Tears started to well in Hillary's eyes as she walked briskly back to the house. She could have done something. She should have done something. She should have reported Keith to the police. She should have stepped in. She could have stopped this. She could have saved Dottie's life. And little Tommy.

Hillary reached the house and went in through the back. No one seemed to be around. The kitchen was strangely quiet for the time of day. Hillary didn't stop to look around. She raced up to her room. She needed to pack her things. She wouldn't be able to move everything right away. She'd pack enough for a few days and would have to come back. But she wasn't staying here. As she shoved clothing into her bag, with no consideration for what she was actually packing, she realized she had to give notice to her landlord. She stopped and walked out of the room, heading for the back stairs. She wasn't thinking anymore. Hillary walked past Robert's door without even a glance. She jogged down the stairs, back into the kitchen.

"Good afternoon, dear," Beatrice greeted her, a bit surprised. "I didn't expect to see you in this time of day."

Hillary didn't answer. She continued through the kitchen and to the basement stairs. Hillary didn't pause to gather her courage this time. She didn't need to. Instead she proceeded directly down the stairs. As she reached the bottom step, a sudden crash stopped her in her tracks.

"God damnit! I thought I told you not to make me this slop anymore," a male voice shouted. The voice was in a rage like Hillary never heard before. The male continued yelling but the words became undiscernible through his rage. What little she could make out was nothing but cursing. And then Hillary heard it. The woman, crying.

Hillary couldn't process it. Was she imagining the sound she just heard? How was this possible? Dottie was dead. She read the article about the accident. But she distinctly heard a woman's voice sobbing as Keith raged on.

"Please stop," came the pleading voice.

"You think you're ever going to get out of here? You think you're ever going to leave me?" he shouted. "They'll take you out of here in a damn body bag before I let that happen. You're not going anywhere, you bitch." This was followed by the sound of something hitting a wall. It sounded like Keith shoved her. The woman cried out. Then everything went quiet. Hillary remained motionless, still unable to comprehend what she was hearing. She heard more sounds, thudding like something being kicked repeatedly.

Hillary reached for her pocket to find the article on her phone again only to realize she left it in her room. None of this made any sense.

"Get up," barked the male voice. "I said get up." There was no respond from the female voice. "Fine, just lay there then. At least then you'll be quiet and I don't have to listen to your goddamn nagging for a little while. Stupid bitch always riding my ass. Nothing ever good enough for you, is it?"

Hillary felt the panic rise. He had beaten her unconscious. She could still do something to help. Dottie wasn't dead. She was still here. It didn't make any sense, but Hillary had to act. And she had to do it right now. The article must have gotten it wrong somehow. Maybe it was the other driver who died in the accident. But right now, Dottie was lying unconscious on the other side of the door in front of her and she had to do something.

Hillary stepped forward and grabbed the knob. It turned. Keith forgot to lock the door. Before she realized what she was doing, she opened the door and rushed inside.

"What the hell?!" Keith yelled in shock. He was laying on a dilapidated looking sofa. "What the fuck are you doing barging in here?!"

Hillary looked around wildly for Dottie on the floor. She left the door standing open as she rushed further into the apartment.

"Where is she?" Hillary demanded, finally looking at Keith.

"What the hell are you talking about and what do you think you're doing in my apartment?" he shouted back at her.

"Dottie," Hillary responded, "where is she?"

"Who the hell is Dottie?" Keith demanded, finally getting up from the sofa. As he got up, Hillary registered the television was on. There was an ad playing across the screen. Keith was shuffling toward her now.

"Your wife, Dottie," Hillary responded, starting to faulter. Hillary finally took in the scene of the room around her. There was no one else here.

"My what? What the hell are you talking about?" Keith demand, still shuffling heavily toward her.

Suddenly, the television blared. It was an old movie Hillary didn't immediately recognize. But the male voice she heard, as the film started up from a commercial break was immediately recognizable as the voice she had been hearing whenever she'd heard the fighting in the basement.

"But I thought," Hillary stammered as she realized it was the television she had been hearing. "I just assumed."

"You better get yourself the hell out of here," Keith growled at her as he got closer.

Hillary turned on her heel, rushed out the door, leaving it standing open. She raced back up the basement stairs.

"Is everything alright, dear?" Beatrice called after her as Hillary rushed back through the kitchen and up the back stairs. Hillary didn't hear her as she dashed back to her room. She had to find her phone. She had to call Rachel about the article. None of this made any sense.

28

Hillary rushed into her room, slamming the door, finding her phone on the table next to her computer. She pulled up the texts from Rachel. Rachel sent the article in a series of screenshots. Hillary tried to slow her breathing down. She needed to think clearly. The photo on her screen was definitely of Dottie and Tommy. They were standing on the front steps of the Maple Street house. The photo was black and white, but it was clearly Dottie. Same perfectly sculpted, dark hair. The dress was even similar to the one she had been wearing whenever Hillary saw her. On looking more closely, she realized it was the same dress Dottie was always wearing. An A-line that fluffed out gracefully from her tiny waist and just skimmed her knees. And little Tommy with his bright, exaggerated smile. A button-down shirt neatly tucked into a pair of pants that looked just a little worn around the knees. The same outfit he always seemed to be wearing. It was them. Hillary was absolutely sure of it. But the caption clearly stated it was a submitted photo, taken some time in 1950.

Hillary set her phone down and started pacing, trying to process what had just happened in the basement. She heard the yelling. She heard the abusive language. The sound of someone being beaten. Someone had been shoved into a wall and slid to the floor. She was sure she heard someone being kicked repeatedly. The woman had been left unconscious. But when she'd opened the door. Did she really open the door and rush into Keith's apartment? Was she completely crazy? There had been no one there but Keith. Keith wasn't married. There was no little boy living in the apartment. It was just Keith; gross and disgusting. But he wasn't abusing his wife. And he hadn't killed her. He was just watching some old, violent movie. Beatrice had been indifferent to the sounds of fighting coming from the basement because it was just a movie Keith watched. Dr. Immerman and Evelyn didn't know Dottie or Tommy because they didn't live in the basement. There was no one living in the basement but Keith. Hillary was shocked out of her racing thoughts by the sound of a knock at her door.

"Hillary is everything alright?" came Evelyn's voice. Evelyn. She could talk to Evelyn. She would know what was going on. Help her make sense of all this. Evelyn had been researching the house. The family who used to live here. Hillary hurried to open the door to her. "Are you okay? You rushed past me so fast just now, you nearly knocked me over," Evelyn said

"I'm fine," Hillary responded quickly. "But I need to show you something." She grabbed Evelyn's arm and pulled her into the room. Evelyn stumbled forward. "You've been researching the family that used to own the house, right?" Evelyn seemed taken aback at Hillary's rambling. "Evelyn, your research. It's about the family who used to live here, right?" Hillary demanded again, growing impatient.

"Hillary, why don't you come sit? You really need to calm down," Evelyn said, moving closer to Hillary and trying to guide her to sit on the edge of the bed. Hillary resisted grabbing her phone from her table. Evelyn finally moved Hillary to the edge of the bed and got her to sit down. Evelyn pulled out her desk chair and perched across from her. "Take a deep breath and tell me what has you so upset."

Hillary let out a long breath in annoyance. It did nothing to calm her. She tapped on her phone screen to find the screenshot from Rachel.

"My friend Rachel sent me this article," Hillary explained, holding out her phone to Evelyn. "Dottie. Dottie and her son, Tommy, were killed in an accident a few days ago. Or at least I thought they were. I thought Keith killed them. He's been abusing Dottie. He yells at her and hits her. He's horrible. But then I went downstairs just now. And I heard him. He was yelling and shouting at Dottie and he beat her. But I went into his apartment, because I couldn't let him get away with it. But there was no one there. It was just Keith and he was watching some movie."

Evelyn's brow knitted in confusion, trying to process everything Hillary just said. She didn't look at the phone screen Hillary was holding out to her.

"Hillary, what are you talking about? Keith isn't married. There's no one but him living in the basement," Evelyn explained. "I think he did time for embezzlement or something. But he's never killed anyone."

"I know," Hillary said emphatically. "But I met a woman and her little boy in the kitchen a few times. And she said something about needing to get the house cleaned up or dinner on the table and she went down the basement."

Evelyn looked at her in confusion. She didn't know how to respond. She waited, hoping Hillary would go on.

"And then when I would go down to the basement to pay my rent, I would hear him. Keith. Yelling and shouting and throwing things. He was abusing her. But she was never down there in the first place. He doesn't have a wife. And there is no little boy living down there. So, who is this?" Hillary waived her phone at Evelyn again. She was still holding it out.

Evelyn took the phone out of Hillary's hand and studied the screenshot for a minute. "Where did you say you got this article from?"

"My friend Rachel sent it to me. But it's just screenshots. I know that's her," Hillary insisted. "That's the woman who was in the kitchen. And her little boy. His name is Tommy and he's six." Evelyn studied the screen.

"Hillary, this article is about an accident Dorothy Brown was involved in back in 1951. Her parents owned this house. She grew up here. And that's her son, Tommy. But they were killed in the accident. Come with me. I'll show you the full article. It has the date on it so you can see it."

Evelyn handed Hillary her phone back. She got up from her chair and headed for the door. Hillary took a last glance at the photo on her phone. She tossed it on her bed as she got up to follow Evelyn.

29

Hillary shifted nervously as Evelyn paged through a file folder she retrieved from the table next to an oversized chair near the windows. Hillary glanced out the windows. The view from Evelyn's room looked out over the back gardens.

"Here it is," Evelyn said, pulling a document from the folder, passing it to Hillary. "I found this during winter break. It should be the same article your friend sent you."

Hillary took the pages in both hands. She looked at it, but she couldn't focus enough to read. Hillary's eyes fixed on the photo. It was the same one from the screenshot on her phone. Dottie and Tommy, smiling together on the front steps of the Maple Street house. Hillary shifted again.

"Here, why don't you sit down. I'll put the lamp on for you," Evelyn gestured toward the oversized chair and then switched on the lamp on the table. Hillary sat down, nervously.

Evelyn pulled another document from another file. She must have been keeping backup copies of her research documents because the article she retrieved looked to be the same one Hillary had in her hands. Hillary calmed herself as best she could. She looked at the top of the page. There was a heading from a local newspaper that no longer existed, as far as Hillary knew. Or at least she wasn't familiar with it. If it was still operating, it was under a different name. Hillary took in the date on the article. It was definitely from 1951. Hillary started reading, finally able to focus. Evelyn sat across from her, on another chair. She glanced through the article quickly but now she sat, not saying anything, watching as Hillary read the article. Hillary looked up at her when she's finished.

"See, Dorothy Brown, or Dottie, as you called her, died in a car crash back in 1951. She fell in love with a Captain who was boarding here, with her parents. From what I've been able to piece together from articles and some old diaries, they planned to run away together. Unfortunately, her abusive husband discovered her plans to leave him and cut her break lines. She thought her husband had done something to the Captain and was racing to find him when she crashed. She and her son were killed on impact."

Hillary stared down at the papers in her hands, taking this all in.

"I don't understand," Hillary finally said, quietly.

"Hillary, what you saw in the kitchen wasn't real. I've never been a believer in spirits or haunted houses. Maybe you read something about the house and stress caused you to think you saw something. But Keith isn't married, and he doesn't have a son. According to her diaries, Dorothy was being abused by her husband and he was having affairs. But she wasn't married to Keith."

"No, that's not what I meant," Hillary said. She didn't say anything else.

"What is it you don't understand?" Evelyn asked her gently.

"The article is cut off at the bottom. It doesn't say anything about the other driver," Hillary said still studying the page in her hands.

"Oh that. The Brown family had been very wealthy, and they were very well known in this area. The library at JC was funded by an endowment from William Brown Senior. That would be Dorothy's grandfather. After the accident, her parents were so devastated, they abandoned the house and left the area. It sat vacant until Keith bought it, at an auction," Evelyn explained.

"But why isn't there anything in here about who was in the other car?" Hillary asked. She kept her eyes down. She couldn't bring herself to look up at Evelyn. She could feel the compassion in Evelyn's voice.

"Well, the family was very well-known, and the local papers would often leave out details when they published articles about them. The Browns made a lot of financial investments in the town and they donated money to a lot of local causes. The papers were not about to publish anything that wasn't entirely focused on the Browns. And you would never find anything written that wasn't flattering to the family."

Hillary remained still in the chair as she listened to Evelyn. Her embarrassment over her outburst was starting to melt away but it was being replaced by something else. A feeling of dread. Something Evelyn said about why Dottie had been out that night. What she was planning to do. Her fear that her husband had done something. There was another question she needed to ask Evelyn, but she couldn't bring herself to ask it. Part of her already knew the answer but she didn't want to hear it. She didn't want to be right. This couldn't be happening. Not to her. Hillary finally looked up at Evelyn. They watched each other for a long moment.

"Are you okay?" Evelyn finally asked. "You've had quite a shock."

"She fell in love with a Captain," Hillary finally said.

"Right, the family took in a returned, wounded soldier who came back from Korea. Dorothy came to visit her parents not long after he moved in. According to her diaries, she fell in love with him," Evelyn explained. Hillary could taste the bitter flavor of bile rising in the back of her throat.

"What was his name?" Hillary asked.

"What was whose name?" Evelyn asked.

"The Captain," Hillary responded.

"Oh, umm, I don't remember off hand," Evelyn said. "It took me a long time to find anything about him. There was an article with a photo when he first moved in. It's rather ironic actually. He went out looking for her the same night Dorothy was out looking for him. But finding anything about him took ages. I was getting so frustrated. He wasn't even named in the article about the accident."

"The accident," asked Hillary.

"Right, it was the Captain Dorothy hit head on that night. But he wasn't named in the article. All it says there was that someone was taken from the scene to a local hospital. I spent weeks trying to track down who he was. Nothing I found, for the longest time, made any mention of his name." Hillary stopped listening to Evelyn's rambling about her research process. "I finally found him though." The pride in Evelyn's voice at finally locating the Captain's identity only made Hillary feel worse.

"Evelyn," Hillary finally interrupted, looking up at her, "what was the Captain's name?"

Evelyn studied her a second, not registering why the Captain would be of so much interest to Hillary. She had long forgotten the mysterious neighbor Hillary insisted was living in the room, next to the bathroom. They hadn't talked about him in ages. Evelyn knew nothing about Hillary trying to introduce her to the friend who came to visit from somewhere out west. Hillary hadn't told her about her embarrassment when she'd finally poured her heart out to him, only to be rejected. Evelyn didn't understand why Hillary was so insistent about knowing who the Captain was. Evelyn looked down at her own copy of the article. She turned a few pages. She thought she kept everything related to the accident together. The next pages were Dorothy Brown's obituary and that of her son. The whole thing was so incredibly sad. She turned the next page.

"Here it is," Evelyn said skimming over the next obituary in the stack. "It should be a few pages back in the pages you have there."

Hillary turned the pages, past Dottie's obituary and Tommy's. Her hands shook as she turned the next page. She glanced over the obituary. There was a photo of a handsome, clean cut young man with raven hair. The face in the grainy, sepia photo was unmistakable. It was Robert.

Epilogue

Evelyn smiled as she typed out the last punctuation. "The face in the grainy, sepia photo was unmistakable. It was Robert." Her research came together brilliantly, if she did say so herself. Her novel was finally finished. She clicked save on the document and closed her laptop, sitting back in her chair with a giddy satisfaction.

Evelyn glanced at her phone, tempted to post about this accomplishment or maybe text her best friend, Sarah. But this was a moment that needed to be savored. Evelyn got up from her desk, slipped on a jacket and tucked her keys in her pocket. The crisp Spring air felt fresh and clean on her face as she stepped out of her apartment. Evelyn breathed deep as she strolled leisurely along the avenue. What an amazing feeling! No more late nights, straining for every last ounce of inspiration she could find to keep up with her writing goals. She knew she had plenty of editing to do in the next week or so, before she would be ready to submit her manuscript. But that wouldn't take much time. She'd get to it later. All she wanted right now was a really good cup of coffee to celebrate.

The snow finally melted, and the world was beginning to green. She soaked it in. The warmth of the sun felt good on her face, despite the chilly Spring air. A line came to mind, something she would write later. She pulled out her phone and wrote it down before she forgot it. Then she tucked her phone back away and continued her walk. This was the first time she'd taken for herself since she'd started this project or so it seemed. She was determined to absorb every moment of this beautiful day.

As Evelyn walked, she glanced around at the historic homes. The coffee shop was still a few blocks away, but she decided to take a quick detour. She had to have another look at the house that was her muse for the book. She turned and picked up her pace a little. It was only a few blocks out of her way. She'd found the house at random, searching real estate listings in the area. And when she saw it, it was like falling in love. That feeling. That sense that this is it. She turned the next corner and continued on. She spotted the white picket fence about half a block away. She could picture the image, from her writing, drifting into her mind's eye. A young child, in a simple cotton dress and pale blond curls. Dottie, as a little girl, was clear in her mind. Her pace slowed as she got closer, coming to a stop across the street from the house. The street was quiet; no one was around to see her staring at the house.

Evelyn could imagine Dr. Immerman, sitting in a wing backed chair, in the study on first floor. Or fingering out a melody on a piano in the corner. She glanced at the second story turret windows. She could picture Hillary, looking out the windows and on to the street, obsessing over her unrequited love. Hillary was based on a blend of her interns at the library. But for the most part, she was a lot like Nina. In fact, it was really Nina's face she imagined as she thought of Hillary sitting at the window, reflecting on her writing or obsessing over her mysterious, handsome neighbor down the hall. Evelyn smiled.

She allowed herself a few more minutes to imagine the characters of her story in the vacant house with the for sale sign out front. The neighborhood was starting to come to life, and she realized she needed to move on. Plus, there was that celebratory coffee to get to. She took a last, long look. Maybe someday she'd own the house on Maple Street, she mused to herself as she walked on.

Glossary

Bar Mitzvah (noun) – a religious initiation ceremony of a Jewish boy who has reached the age of 13 and is regarded as ready to observe religious precepts and is eligible to take part in public worship.

Bubbe (noun) – The Yiddish term for grandmother.

Chica (noun) – The Spanish term for girl.

Chuppah (noun) – A canopy beneath which Jewish marriage ceremonies are performed.

Kiddush (noun) – A ceremony of prayer and blessing over wine proceeding a Sabbath meal.

Mahjong (noun) – A Chinese game played, usually by four people with 136 or 144 rectangular pieces called tiles.

Seder (noun) – A Jewish ritual service and ceremonial dinner for the first night of Passover.

Shabbat (noun) – The Hebrew term for the Jewish Sabbath.

Sufganiyot (noun) – The Hebrew name for jelly doughnuts traditionally served during Hanukkah.

Yelda (noun) – The Hebrew term for girl.

www.ingramcontent.com/pod-product-compliance
Lightning Source LLC
Chambersburg PA
CBHW032143170626
46808CB00006B/2347